Stumbling Into Forever

STUMBLING THROUGH LIFE BOOK TWO

MOLLY O'HARE

Dedication

This book is dedicated to all the Holly's out there looking for your Ben. He's out there. And, for all the Holly's that have their Ben's, Rock on!

Also, in good old Molly O'Hare fashion, you are amazing. You are beautiful, you are special. You are a mother fucking Unicorn. Rock your stuff, because no one is just like you and that's amazing.
Go forth and keep kicking ass.
And if no one has told you today, I will: You are fucking perfect.

Xoxo

Stumbling Into Forever

STUMBLING THROUGH LIFE BOOK TWO

MOLLY O'HARE

Chapter One

"DROP THAT DONUT RIGHT NOW, Waffles, or so help me, I'm gonna murder you *and* enjoy it!"

Ben Richman heard his wife, Holly, yelling from their kitchen. With a chuckle and a shake of his head, he removed their cat Twitch from his lap and made his way through the house to investigate.

What has she gotten herself into now? A smirk spread across his face.

"Don't you run away from me, Waffles! That's mine and you know it!" The growl Ben heard coming from Holly had him laughing. Leave it to her to argue with a dog. Then again, this was Lord Waffles they were talking about. Arguing with him was a must, as Ben had come to find out since meeting Holly and her overly opinionated, high and mighty Corgi.

As Ben rounded the corner, he saw his oh so graceful wife running around the kitchen island chasing after their dog.

The same dog that just so happened to have Holly's last donut in his mouth.

As Waffles ran past the spot where Ben stood, the dog had

the gall to eye him, almost begging to get the crazy lady to stop chasing him.

Figures.

Ben rolled his eyes. He'd be lying if he didn't say there was a part of him that wanted to watch the catastrophe he was sure was about to happen. Everyone knew whatever Waffles wanted, Waffles got, and if that meant destroying everything in his wake, or taking his mother's last donut, even though he knew he'd be staring death in the eyes, he'd do it. Everyone was beneath Waffles, and that dog made sure they knew it. Including his mother, who clearly wanted that last donut bad enough, she'd fight for it.

Ben shook his head with a sigh. As much as he'd like to watch the chaos there was another part of him, a bigger part, that wanted to make sure no one ended up on the floor in a pile of blood because they banged their head against the countertop.

And by no one, he meant Holly.

Better get this over with. "Grace, stop chasing him before you end up on your ass." Ben laughed as he stepped into the kitchen.

Ben had learned a thing or two after being married to Holly for the better part of a year, and there was no doubt in his mind what was coming next.

Prepared, Ben strategically placed his hands out in front of him.

Within seconds, Holly came barreling into his arms at full speed. Although Ben was ready, he somehow lost his footing, causing them to cascade to the floor with a loud oomph.

"Ahh!" Holly screamed as they landed.

The moment they were on the floor she tried to jump off him. You know that fight-or-flight instinct? Ben wasn't having any of it though. He held onto her hips, keeping her locked in place on top of him.

"What on earth am I going to do with you, Grace?" Ben chuckled, as he helped Holly straighten herself so she was now straddling his waist.

"Where in the world did you freakin' come from?" Holly huffed while she pushed her auburn hair out of her face. She didn't wait for an answer as she scanned the room for any sign of his holiness.

As if on cue, Lord Waffles walked past them with the donut in his mouth and an extra pep in his step.

Holly growled as she narrowed her eyes at the betraying bastard. The moment Waffles shot her a wink, Ben had to stop her from lunging.

Ben's brows shot to the ceiling when Waffles winked at him too.

Waffles freaking *winked* at him.

No matter how many times he'd seen Waffles demand his peasants listen to him, Ben still couldn't believe it. For a dog, he sure did have a lot of quirks. In the name of veterinary medicine, maybe he should study him, possibly resea–

"You knew that was mine!" Holly made a second lunge for Waffles as he happily chomped on his treasure, taunting her.

Thank God Ben's reflexes were sharp—that's what happens after spending years wrestling Rottweilers. And clearly, Holly couldn't be trusted not to strangle their dog right now.

In one swift movement, Ben grabbed Holly's hips, flipping her onto her back and under him with ease. "It's too late now, Grace. You wouldn't want it after he's slobbered all over it anyway."

"Says you!" Holly glared at him. "That was my last peanut butter and glazed donut. I've been saving it until I reached my word count. He knew that! We talked about it in great detail when I was struggling to hit my next two thousand words. He did this on purpose." Holly's eyes snapped to Waffles who was swallowing the last bite before licking his lips. "I'm gonna remember this the next time you need something." She glared at him one last time before she threw her head back onto the floor in defeat. "That was my donut."

The pout that spread across Holly's mouth had Ben laughing.

And he wondered where Waffles got his flair for the dramatics?

"I'll buy you more." He laughed, kissing Holly lightly on the lips. As Ben looked down at his wife, a smile ran across his face. He still couldn't believe how lucky he was to have found Holly. Even though that meeting involved her getting hit in the face with a rogue Frisbee, which now knowing Holly, wasn't all that surprising. She was, after all, a master at tripping on thin air, falling over, and if you looked up the word klutz in the dictionary, you'd see a picture of her, with the title walking disaster under it. But to him, she was absolutely perfect in every way. From her lush hips down to the deep hunter green of her eyes.

Holly was made for him.

"It won't be the same," Holly groaned as she pushed the palm of her hand to his chest and gave a nudge. "And stop calling me Grace! You jumped in front of me. It was *your* fault I ended up crashing into you. Not mine. What was I supposed to do? You came out of freakin' nowhere!"

Ben threw his head back and burst out laughing, causing Holly to let out a growl, which only made him laugh harder. "I don't know, Grace. How about stop?"

"As if I could stop. Once this load starts a-movin', nothing is stopping it."

"Excuse me?" Ben's brows shot to the ceiling.

Panic flashed through Holly's eyes.

Good. After all this time you should know better than to say shit like that.

Before Ben could say anything more, Ripley came bouncing into the kitchen, with Twitch right on her tail.

"Oh, oh, Ripley, baby girl, come save your momma," Holly cooed at their other dog, Ripley, their Australian shepherd.

Ripley quickly made her way over to Holly's face and started licking. "That's not saving me!" Holly squirmed as she did her best to avoid the onslaught of kisses coming from Ripley.

That's when Ben felt something nudge his arm. He looked down to see Twitch—rightly named so because of the slight twitch he has in his head from some punk kid poisoning him when he was a kitten.

Twitch jumped onto Holly's chest, trying to lick her face just as Ripley was, making Ben laugh again.

Somewhere along the lines, Twitch had taken to Ripley like she was his own mother and converted himself into being a dog.

Where Ripley went, Twitch went.

Whatever Ripley did, Twitch did.

Ben's heart warmed at the memories of Ripley and Waffles play fighting and Twitch trying to jump in and hold his own. The play fighting only lasted a few seconds before Ripley would grab Twitch in her mouth and take him away from the fight.

Go figure. Protective. Just like Holly.

Although right now, Holly looked more like she wanted to throttle Waffles rather than protect him.

Twitch looked at Ripley before assessing they were still kissing their mother. So, he dove back in.

At this point, Ben was positive all their animals were certifiably insane. And with their ringmaster, Lord Waffles, with plans of world domination, calling most of the shots he'd given up trying to make any sense of it.

But he wouldn't have it any other way.

Life was always an adventure between their pets and Holly.

Oh, and Ben couldn't forget Mildred. Holly's completely inappropriate older coworker at the local library. Whenever Mildred was around, things *always* got interesting.

Ben pushed himself off Holly before grabbing onto her arms yanking her to her feet. "Up you go, Grace."

"I'm gonna put arsenic in your dinner tonight."

"That'd be a welcomed taste with your cooking." At Holly's narrowed eyes he barked out a laugh. "Come on. You know it's true. Sexy, talented, outspoken, kindhearted, feisty, best writer in the world you are... a chef you ain't. Or do you want me to bring up the time you almost burned the house down when you tried to make chicken tenders?"

Another growl came from Holly. "That wasn't my fault!"

"Yes, my bad, that's right. It was the chicken's fault."

"Damn right it was! Plus, I was only trying to be nice and feed you and John 'cause you guys were working hard moving my crap in."

"Oh, we got a break from moving your shit in when we had to call the fire department." Ben smirked at her angry eyes and thinned lips.

"Am I ever going to live that down?"

"No." Ben's eyes twinkled with amusement. "Hey, at least I'm not as bad as John."

Annoyed Holly jerked herself away from him and grabbed her bag. "You and John can kiss my ass."

When she started for the front door Ben hollered after her, "Where do you think you're going?"

From over her shoulder, Holly shot him an evil look. "Out to get more donuts."

At the word 'donut' Waffles ran to Holly's side and started

jumping. Well, if you can consider whatever Waffles does with his tiny little legs jumping.

"Not for you!" Holly sidestepped Waffles shooting her glare from Ben to their dog.

Holly almost made it all the way to the front door without an incident.

Almost.

As she moved through the hallway, she tripped over an invisible crack and stumbled. Without looking back at Ben, she quickly righted herself before blowing her hair out of her face.

Ben did a quick assessment of her to make sure she was okay. When he realized she was fine, he let out a laugh.

As Ben opened his mouth to tell her to bring him back some donuts too, Holly did what she was known for. She tripped over the entranceway and nearly fell right out of the door.

Ben had to bite back his joy as his smile spread from ear to ear. *Never a dull moment.*

Holly straightened herself with a huff as she hiked her bag higher onto her shoulder. Once she was composed, she turned to face him with narrowed eyes. "Not. A. Word."

Ben held his hands up in surrender as he bit his lip, trying and failing to keep from laughing.

The second Holly turned from him and stomped out of the door, he shouted, "And you wonder why I'll never stop calling you Grace!"

Chapter Two

HOLLY PLOPPED the box of donuts onto her desk as she threw herself into her chair with a sigh.

Universe, if you love me at all, please let today be an easy day.

"What did ya bring me?" Mildred, Holly's coworker, made her way toward Holly with her eyes honed in on the box.

Holly had to do a double take. Seriously, like where in the hell had Mildred come from? For an old woman, she sure was fast.

Before Holly could even register Mildred had her sights on Holly's delectable goodies, the old hag had one of the donuts shoved into her mouth.

"Damn, this is good," Mildred mumbled around the food.

Holly's eyes widened for a brief second, trying to stop her brain from short-circuiting. Wasn't it a known rule older women needed to watch their sugar intake? Holly watched as Mildred chomped on the donut.

Clearly not.

Holly rolled her eyes before opening the box to grab a

peanut butter and glazed donut. "I know. That's why I bought them."

"Mine!" Mildred snatched the donut from Holly's hand bringing it to her mouth before taking a big bite. "You don't need any sweets when you got that hunk of burning man meat to satisfy all your cravings." Mildred took another bite of the donut as Holly watched in horror.

I'll kill her! No one would blame me!

"Cat got your tongue there, missy?" Mildred winked. "Or, should I say dog got your tongue?" She licked the remainder of the peanut butter glaze off her fingers with a pop. "You get it? 'Cause you have dogs."

Do not kill your coworker. Do not kill your coworker. Holly narrowed her eyes at her. "I also have a cat. You know, Mildred, you are so unbelievably lucky I already ate one on the way here. If I hadn't, you'd be a dead woman." Holly opened the box and blindly grabbed for another tasty treat making sure not to break eye contact with the old hag.

"Are you trying to intimidate me?" Mildred placed one of her hands on her hips.

"Is it working?"

"Not on your life, little miss. Where do you think that stare came from?" She pointed at herself. "I've perfected it over the years."

Giving up, Holly moved her eyes to the donut she'd grabbed. *Why the hell didn't I just buy a dozen of the peanut butter ones?* Holly rolled her eyes. *That's what I get for trying to be more health conscious.*

"What are you doing here so early, anyway?" Mildred asked, plopping herself onto the corner of the desk. "Ole Benny boy not performing as he should? Did you know they make this pill that—"

"Oh, for the love of all things."

"That's what I'm saying. If Mr. Hotness has a problem in the love department, I know a guy."

"Eww." Holly shoved her fingers in her ears as she shook her head. "I don't want to hear that."

Mildred held up her hands in surrender. "Fine. I'll call Ben myself and tell him." She picked up the phone, but Holly snatched it back.

"How do you go from zero to ten thousand in the span of two seconds?" Holly placed the phone back onto the receiver.

"It's a gift." Mildred eyed the donut box. "Ask my husband."

"I'll be sure to mention to him how you need to be placed in a facility under intense supervision."

Mildred shrugged before reaching for another treat.

I should have known better than to bring them here.

"If Benny isn't the problem then what's got you all in a huff?"

"I'm stuck."

Mildred arched her brow. "To the chair? Do I need to call the fire department? Remember the last time we had to call them when you tried to heat up leftovers. Oh God, they were mouthwatering."

Holly could see drool form in the corner of Mildred's mouth as a faraway look washed over her eyes. "Geez, Mildred, how does your husband handle you?"

"With rough hands, if I'm lucky."

"For the love of—" Holly stopped before taking a deep breath to calm herself. "Mildred, I'm stuck in my story. I've been going back and forth for weeks trying to get it right, but everything I do is a disaster. I don't know which way to turn."

The old bat scrutinized her for a few seconds. "Are you sure it's not Ben and his dong?"

Holly jumped from her seat. "Why do I even bother talking to you?"

"You love me, and you know I can help."

Holly started making her way to the book return ignoring Mildred. She should have known better than to believe walking away from her would have stopped the conversation.

"You're unsettled," Mildred remarked.

Holly spun to face her. "What?"

"Missy, do not *what* me like that." Mildred placed her hands on her hips. "I'm telling you, I can see it in your eyes. You're unsettled. Something is missing from your life."

"My life is perfect," Holly protested. "Well, other than the missing words, I couldn't ask for anything more."

"Liar." Mildred turned on her heel and started making her way back to the desk.

"I am not!" Ignoring the fact Mildred was chomping on another one of the donuts Holly turned back to her task. "I am not a liar. My life *is* perfect," she mumbled.

And it was.

She had Ben by her side. He was the love of her life. She still hadn't quite figured out why a hunk like him was interested in a world champion klutz machine like her, but at this point, she learned to accept it. Their home was filled with love. Even if Lord Waffles felt he owned the place and only *allowed* the rest of them to live there, she loved it. She had Twitch, Ripley, and Ben there.

Stupid old woman. Holly looked back toward the desk and noticed Mildred was gone. "I bet she ate the last of my donuts too."

Would it be crazy if I got a lockbox and put donuts in it? She pondered the idea for a moment before dismissing it. *Man, this writer's block is making me crazy. I doubt other aspiring authors argue with themselves over donuts. Who does that? Oh yeah, me. I do that.*

Holly felt her phone vibrate in her pocket.

She sighed.

For some reason her agitation was in full swing. *Maybe I'm PMSing.*

With a quick glance at the screen, she answered. "Hey, Dad."

"Pumpkin, how are you?"

"I'm doing good, Dad. What's up?" Holly took a cleansing breath. Whatever was bugging her was her problem, not her father's. She wasn't going to take it out on Henry.

"Oh, nothing. Why does something have to be up for me to call my daughter? Can't an old man just want to say hi?"

Guilt rushed through her. "Yes, Dad, of course. I didn't mean to imply anything." Holly grabbed one of the books and placed it on the shelf. *Great, now I feel like a jerk.* "What are you doing?"

"I'm talking to you of course."

"Dad..."

"Okay, fine. I wanted to see if you and Ben were free to come over for dinner tonight?"

Holly felt the start of a headache coming. "I planned on coming over after work tonight you know that," she reminded him.

"Yes, I know you were planning on coming over. But I want to extend the invitation to Ben and the pups."

Holly eyed the phone suspiciously. "Okay fine, I'll call Ben on my lunch break. He took Ripley and Waffles to work today."

"Good, good."

"You sure you're okay?" It had only been two days since she saw her father last, but with his disabilities, anything could have happened in her absence. Her worry started to rise. What if something had happened? What if he was trying to fix something in the house and fell and hurt himself? What if he was calling from the floor with a broken hip? What if he needed more food? What if—

"Of course, I am..." Holly could swear she heard him growl. *"Now, I'm going to hang up and let you get back to work."*

Holly's brows knitted together. "Sorry, Dad. I guess I'm in a mood or something." She sighed. "We'll be over later. I know Ben will want to come."

"Perfect. Oh, and Pumpkin?"

Just like that Holly's eye began to twitch. "Yeah, Dad?"

"Do you think Ben would be able to make his spicy chicken tonight?"

Oh, for the love of all things! She knew her father better than to just have a quick "how you doing" phone call in the middle of the day. *First Waffles eats my donut, then Mildred eats my replacements, and now my dad wants nothing to do with me, but wants Ben to make him his favorite food.* She bit back a growl. Holly shook her head as she tapped her finger on one of the books. "Yeah, Dad. I'll tell him that's what you're requesting. Is there anything else?"

"Wonderful! Oh, and Holly, please don't make anything. Leave the cooking up to Ben. See you tonight, Pumpkin!"

Holly squeezed her phone a little tighter after the call ended. She took another cleansing breath, trying to ease her annoyance.

Holly had absolutely no idea why everything was getting to her today.

It's all Mildred's fault. Her lips thinned.

Holly quickly sent a text message to Ben letting him know they'd be going to her Dad's for dinner and if he wouldn't mind making his spicy chicken.

She knew Ben would be all for it. He loved hanging out with Henry.

Holly put her phone in her back pocket and picked up the last return book before placing it on the shelf.

Unfortunately for her, the frustration she'd been feeling

reared its ugly head in her movements. She slammed the book onto the shelf harder than she needed to.

Within seconds the shelf collapsed, causing all the books to cascade onto the floor. "You have got to be freakin' kidding me!" Holly threw her hands over her head before she walked away.

Today was not her day.

She walked back to the desk with Mildred's "You're a liar" ringing through her head. When Holly reached for her box of donuts, she noticed a book placed on top of them.

When she saw the title, it was like a sucker punch to the gut.

Chapter Three

"Tell me, how are the newlyweds doing?" Henry, Holly's father asked as they sat down for dinner that evening with Lord Waffles sitting at his feet begging for any scrap Grandpa would send his way.

"Are you going to ask us that every day, Dad?" Holly asked, sitting in the spot across from her father.

"Probably." Henry took a bite of his chicken. "Ben, this is outstanding, thank you. It gets better and better each time you make it."

A whine came from under the table. When Ben leaned over to see who it was, he saw Waffles at Henry's feet with big round eyes staring back at him.

"You know you're not supposed to have table food," Ben remarked, looking at the pup. "Plus, you wouldn't like it, anyway. It's spicy." Ben popped a piece of food in his mouth, winking at their dog.

Waffles gave him the most judgmental side-eye he could muster before turning his nose up. "Jesus, dog, you act like we don't feed you." Ben shook his head.

Waffles answered with a huff before moving his attention to Henry.

You've got to be kidding me.

Ben watched as Waffles placed one of his paws on Henry's left foot. The little shit then had the gall to look up at Holly's dad giving him *sad* eyes.

"Come off it, dude. You're not getting any chicken." Ben looked at his father-in-law. "Don't feed him any. Besides, he's in trouble anyway."

Henry placed his fork back on his plate before moving his good arm down to scratch Waffles behind the ear. "Waffles in trouble? Why he could never be a bad boy," Henry cooed. "Ain't that right, little man?"

"Don't enable him."

Waffles, the jerk that he was, ate up the attention. He even fell onto his back, giving Henry better access for belly rubs.

The second Ben groaned his annoyance, Waffles sent him another evil glare.

Ben shook his head before placing another piece of food in his mouth. "Why can't you be more like your sister? Ripley is at least waiting in the corner."

How has my life come to this?

"Because he's too smart for that," Henry remarked. "He knows where his bread is buttered and that's with Grandpa."

Ben darted his eyes to Holly where all she did was shrug her shoulders. "I've had to deal with this since I got him. *Grandpa* takes his role very seriously." Holly smirked before taking a bite of her own food.

"Yeah, but we can't reward him, especially when he's been an ass. That little shit decided to intimidate a Great Dane today at work. Do you know how hard it is to control one of those massive things?" Ben glared at their Corgi who in return scoffed before turning back to Henry.

"Oh, I'm sure it wasn't Waffles's fault," Henry responded as he continued to scratch the Corgi.

"It was most certainly his fault." Ben narrowed his eyes at the menace. "The client brought her dog in and *Waffles* decided he *needed* to remind everyone who was in charge. As the owner pulled Bruce, who might I add was terrified, into the waiting room, Waffles decided to run from behind the reception area and make himself known. When Bruce noticed him, do you want to know what he did?"

Henry bent shielding Waffles with his arms to coddle him, the best he could with his physical disabilities. "Did the dog attack, Waffles?" Henry asked with concern. Waffles, being the ham he was, had the audacity to cry out as if to tell Henry that's exactly what happened.

"No." Ben rolled his eyes. "On the contrary, Bruce took off running the other way, nearly pulling his owner's arm out of her socket. Then Waffles *chased* him. He freaking chased him all through the waiting room causing chaos to erupt."

"So, you're saying a Great Dane—those big old dogs—was afraid of this little guy?" Ben could see Henry trying to hide his smile.

"That's exactly what I am saying. Who knew a massive guy like that would be terrified to death of a puffed out loaf of bread? I knew Bruce had some issues in the past, but damn."

"Do not call our son a loaf of bread!" Holly exclaimed before glaring at Ben. "He is *not* a loaf of bread."

"My apologies, babe." Ben held his hands in surrender. "I meant to say an oversized potato."

A mischievous smile appeared on Holly's face. "Damn right. And that's Mr. Potato to you." She pointed her finger at him while she absolutely failed to control her amusement.

A loud huff came from Waffles, causing Ben to turn the attention back to him. That's when he saw their Corgi shooting death glares directed right for him and Holly.

"Who's a good Mr. Potato?" Ben mocked, his eyes full of joy.

"You all need to stop being so mean to my grandbaby." Henry took a piece of broccoli off his plate and handed it to the dog. The second Waffles realized it wasn't chicken, he promptly spat the offending food out before turning his glare to Henry.

With a dramatic huff and a rise of his snout, Waffles turned and made his way out of the kitchen. When he got to the start of the hallway, Waffles turned back to glare at all three of them.

With one last huff to inform everyone of his disdain about how he'd been treated, he waddled away.

The room fell silent only for a moment before they all erupted in laughter.

"Aww, poor little guy. Should one of us go out and comfort him?" Henry asked as he picked up his fork to start eating.

"Not it," Holly and Ben said at the exact same time with smiles on their faces, which caused more laughter to burst throughout the room.

Ben, doing his best to control his amusement of the situation looked at Ripley who was sitting patiently at the entrance to the kitchen watching the show.

As she cocked her head to the side, waiting for Ben's command, she realized what he was asking. With her own drawn-out sigh, Ripley slowly made her way out of the kitchen in search of her brother. She only looked back once, which caused Ben to give a small nod of encouragement. Ripley then did something Ben never thought she would do.

Ripley dropped to the floor in a full-on tantrum.

What the hell? I mean I know she's picked up a few things from Waffles, but damn!

Not sure what was happening Ben pushed himself from

the table. That's when Ripley stood before sighing loud enough for everyone to hear before disappearing out of sight.

Holly's mouth fell open, and Henry's eyes were so wide, Ben thought they were going to pop out of his head.

He was also positive his expression mirrored both of theirs.

"Uh, Ben," Holly finally broke the silence, clearly trying to get her bearings. "Did she just throw a hissy fit like a teenager who was just asked to clean up their bedroom?"

Still in disbelief, Ben nodded. "I think she did."

"Not her too!" Holly cried, throwing her hands into the air. "You've got to be kidding me."

"Ripley was never a diva until Waffles showed up." Ben narrowed his eyes at his wife.

"Are you saying this is my fault?" Holly glared back.

"No. I'm saying it's Waffles." Ben darted his eyes to the spot Ripley had just vacated. "That's it. We are separating those two from now on."

Holly nodded. "Agreed."

When did my life become a reality TV show?

Ben pulled his seat back to the table to finish his meal. *Out of sight, out of mind.* As he picked up his fork, he saw Ripley accompanied by Waffles make their way back into the kitchen.

They both simultaneously plopped onto the kitchen floor right next to the entrance.

Ben didn't miss the evil eye still coming from Waffles, though.

He shook his head. Ben was determined to ignore the insanity his life had become.

HOLLY PICKED up a forkful of chicken and shoved it in her mouth. Secretly she was glad her father wanted this for dinner.

It was one of her favorite meals. And after a day like today, she needed the pick me up.

Had she mentioned the same bookshelf fell three more times during her shift? Or how Mildred kept leaving her little surprise books everywhere she turned?

She worried her bottom lip. Leave it to Mildred to throw her world completely upside down.

Holly kept stealing glances at her husband, trying to pick apart what he was thinking. She knew they had talked about having children before but nothing solid.

But now that was all Holly could think about.

The idea of growing a little Richman inside of her made her feel things she never thought were possible.

Now, if she could only get a few seconds to talk to Ben about it.

She pushed around a piece of broccoli on her plate, as she continued worrying her bottom lip. When she looked at Ben again, she noticed him staring at her.

Her heart soared. There was so much love in his eyes, it was almost too much to take.

A warm smile spread across his face the moment their eyes met. Holly was positive it matched her own.

She loved him.

And she was ready.

Ben would be the best dad there could be, other than her own of course. Look at the way Ben handled their fur-babies.

As she stared at him, she couldn't help but imagine a little blue-eyed boy who looked exactly like his daddy on Ben's lap.

She quickly looked away. If she didn't, she probably would have pulled a Holly and blurted it out in front of everyone.

That was not something she wanted to discuss with her father around.

When Ben arched a brow at her, she decided she needed to change gears.

Stay cool. No need to embarrass yourself during dinner. We've got a whole car ride home to talk about it. Think about something else.

Holly turned her attention to her father.

There'd been so many years they'd sat across from each other at this exact same table sharing a meal together. Back then, however, his eyes always held torment and pain.

Now his eyes held a lightness and joy. She wasn't exactly sure what changed in him, but she was grateful for it. Seeing her dad happy filled her heart. She was sure some of it had to do with the fact his bills were no longer hanging over his head, but it was more than that. She liked this new look on him.

Whenever she looked his way now, he'd have his lopsided grin fully on display.

Holly's life had morphed into something she'd never thought she'd be privileged to. Ben, her dad, their animals. All of it. This type of fulfillment was never in the cards for her, but now that she had it, she couldn't help but fantasize about the one thing she knew would make her heart feel one hundred percent full.

I want a baby.

The sucker punch feeling she had earlier in the day returned with a new force. She knew she couldn't wait another moment. It was do or die.

Unfortunately, the second Holly opened her mouth Ben's phone rang.

Dang it!

"This is Ben."

Within seconds, Holly watched as Ben's face paled. All thoughts of their future disappeared as a gut-wrenching feeling of wrong swept through her.

Oh no!

Ben's face contorted as he continued with the call. "Are

you serious, is everything all right? How about the animals?" Ben asked.

Holly was nearly in a full-blown panic. She shot out of her seat knocking her chair onto the floor behind her.

Ben jumped from his seat and started heading to the front door. "I'll be there in a few minutes," Ben said before shoving the phone into the back pocket of his jeans.

"What's going on?" Holly asked, running after him.

"Yeah, son, is everything okay?"

Ben turned back to them, an expression of panic on his face which caused Holly's stomach to sink. She'd never seen this type of dread on Ben before, not even when they were dealing with his psychotic mother.

"Someone broke into the clinic."

Chapter Four

WHEN THE CLINIC appeared in Ben's sights, he realized it was still surrounded by police cars, causing his stomach to churn.

Oh God.

As he heard dogs barking in the background a new wave of dread washed through him.

At least let the animals be okay. The other stuff I can deal with, just please let them be okay.

He pulled into the parking lot and jumped out of the car. From the corner of his eye, he saw Holly right behind him.

When Ben spotted an officer standing outside of the building, he took off in a run. "Can you tell me what's going on?" he asked. Since the officer didn't immediately say anything Ben added, "Can you tell me if Detective William Bower is here? He's a friend of mine."

The officer nonchalantly turned toward Ben. "And you might be?"

"I'm Benjamin Richman. I own this clinic." All the officer did was nod in return.

Jesus fucking Christ. What do I do?

By the look of this guy, it was clearly someone you did not want to piss off. He had a certain presence about him. Maybe it was the muscles upon muscles, or maybe it was his hardened face? He wasn't quite sure. One thing he did know was he should probably go and ask someone else. However, the second he took a step away from the officer in search of someone else, he heard Holly.

"That's all you've got, a freaking nod?" Holly stomped toward them. "You tell us exactly what's going on you big lug. And right now!"

The officer's right brow shot to the sky. "And *you* might be?"

"Are those the only words you know how to say?" Holly spat. "You'd think to be an officer of the law you'd have better communication skills. You tell my husband right now what the hell is going on or I'll—"

"You'll what?" The officer turned his body fully in Holly's direction before crossing his arms over his chest.

Fucking A!

Ben pulled Holly to his side away from the officer who looked like he was about to break something in half, and he was pretty sure that something in half was going to be Holly. Or, you know, he might've been constipated. Either way, he wasn't taking a chance. "Let's try not to piss off Officer..." Ben looked at the officer's badge. "Jones. I don't want to have to bail you out of jail while trying to deal with all of this."

Holly jumped out of Ben's arms, disbelief written all over her face. "Bail *me* out of jail?"

Ben didn't know if it was his adrenaline or whatnot, but the audacity on Holly's face nearly sent him into hysterics.

He bit back his reaction as he took a deep breath. Not the time nor the place.

Leave it to Holly to find a way to calm him and bring him back to reality. And right now, while she practically had her dukes up ready for battle—a battle she would not win against a two hundred plus pound man who could snap her in two— she grounded him. "Relax, Cujo. Let me take care of this."

"You wanna see Cujo, I'll show you Cujo." Holly narrowed her eyes at him as her nostrils flared causing him to hold his hands in surrender, before he turned back to Officer Jones.

"I apologize. We both are a little riled up. Let's start over. Would you be willing to give us some information or at least point me in the direction of someone who can?"

Officer Jones gave him the once-over before nodding.

"Is that all this guy can do?" Holly growled as she pointed her finger at the officer. Ben darted his eyes to her in warning. *Do not get us killed or arrested.*

"What?" Holly arched her brow.

Please give me strength. Any strength. I would take anything at this moment. The universe must've answered him since Officer Jones started walking toward the front door of the clinic. Ben looked back at Holly who shrugged.

Following his cue, they walked behind the officer. When they made it inside of the clinic, his gut twisted into a knot.

It was a disaster.

Chairs from the waiting room were thrown all around. There was glass from the smashed in window everywhere. It was horrifying.

"Bower, the owner's here."

As soon as Ben saw his old friend, relief washed through him. Will turned to face him, a sad expression marring his features. "Ben."

"Will." Ben reached out to shake his hand.

"I know we said we wanted to catch up soon but this was not what I had in mind," Will remarked as he scratched his chin. He turned to Holly. "You must be Ben's wife. Ben mentioned he was getting married the last time we talked."

"Yes." Ben pulled Holly to his side. "This is Holly. You never got to officially meet her."

"It was my fault," Will remarked. "You know when my little girl got sick, it took all my time." Will sheepishly looked away. He didn't have to though. Once Will's daughter was diagnosed with cancer, he and his wife had spent all their time with her. The day of Ben and Holly's wedding Will and his wife Martha were taking their girl in for treatment. There was no fault in that.

"How is she doing?" Ben asked, hoping for the best.

"Better." Will's face lit. "She's in full remission now. The day we got the last results was by far the happiest day of my life." A smile spread across the detective's face. "You know, Ben, I'm sure Martha would love to see you, maybe one day we can have you and your little lady over for dinner one night."

"We'd like that," Ben answered.

"It's nice to finally meet you." Will placed his hand in front of Holly's. "I do wish it was under better circumstances, though."

"You and me both." Holly took his outreached hand and shook it.

"Can you tell us what happened?" Ben asked, while he looked around the room again.

"To be honest, we don't know much. The station got the call when the alarm went off. When officers first arrived on scene, they noticed the window was smashed in. Since veterinarian clinics often get broken into because of the controlled substances they carry, the arriving officers called it in right away."

A cold sweat broke out on the back of Ben's neck. "This was a robbery?"

"It doesn't look that way." Detective Bower scratched his chin again. "From our initial search of the premises, we didn't find any locked cabinets tampered with. Nor did we find any evidence of a robbery. It doesn't seem to appear any money is missing. Although you will need to confirm that for us."

"So, someone just did this to do it?" Holly asked. "Oh God, what about all the animals in the back?" Holly pushed herself through the officers as she finagled her way to the back of the clinic where the boarded animals were along with the ones recovering from recent surgeries.

"Mrs. Richman, this is an active crime scene. You can't go anywhere," Will yelled after her.

Holly clearly didn't care if it was an active investigation or not. She ignored his words as she tore through the clinic.

Screw it!

Ben took off after her. He had the same concerns she did. Especially since he could still hear the dogs barking.

Ben heard Will mumble something under his breath before he followed after them.

Once they all made their way into the back, Ben saw Holly crouched in front of one of the cages which housed a dog who had recently gone through surgery.

"Grace." Ben started walking toward her.

"I know. I know, I just needed to make sure none of them were hurt. Okay?" Quickly she jumped from where she was to the next cage, checking on one of their dogs that was being boarded.

Ben watched as she bounced from cage to cage, confirming all the animals were unharmed.

God, he loved her. All she cared about was making sure the animals were safe. Ben followed suit checking on his patients as he went.

"Grace? I thought you said her name was Holly," Will questioned.

As if on cue, Holly pushed over a step stool to check on a

cat in one of the top cages. In her frantic movements, she missed her footing and started tumbling over.

Ben was at her side in an instant as he caught her in his arms just as he'd done time and time again.

He turned back to Will with Holly cradled in his arms. "Grace is short for her gracefulness."

Will looked at them quizzically but nodded with a smirk.

"Ben, the cameras!" Holly exclaimed as she jumped out of his arms and ran toward his office.

"Do you have surveillance cameras set up?" Will asked.

"We do." Ben followed behind Holly as she made her way into his office.

"I'll have to ask if you could please provide us with a copy of the footage so we can conduct our investigation."

"Of course, Will, anything you need."

"I can't remember what program it is." Holly was bent over the back of Ben's office chair typing away at his computer. Any other time he would have laughed at her *Hollyness*.

Instead, Ben strolled behind her before picking her up into the air and moving her out of his way. "Let me get it open and we'll hand it over to the detective. Right now, we're only in their way."

"I'm never in the way." Holly placed her hand over her heart like she'd been shot.

Holly then darted her eyes to Will whose brow was cocked.

"Okay, fine." She threw her hands up before storming out of the office, leaving a concerned Ben behind. "I know when I'm not wanted."

Ben rolled his eyes. He loved her, but he was one hundred percent going to remind her of this the next time she complained about Waffles and his dramatics.

He couldn't blame her. Hell, if he wasn't as in control as he was, he'd be acting the same way Holly was. Ben turned back to the detective. "Man, Will, it's great to see you again but this is definitely not the way I wanted to reconnect." He rubbed his forehead. "Something like this has never happened to either of us. Why would anyone want to break in here, Will?" Ben shook his head still in disbelief. *How and why did this happen?* "Whatever you need from us we can provide, you know that."

"It's understandable, Ben." He nodded. "This isn't something anyone is prepared for. I'm just glad I was working tonight." He jutted his chin out to the computer. "I'll have my men take it from here, okay?"

"Thank you."

"I know it's going to be a long night getting everything back in order. How about you come to the station tomorrow morning and we can fill out all the paperwork then? Since this is a clinic that has controlled substances, the reports are a tad more tedious. There's no need for you to have to deal with it tonight, though."

"I appreciate that, Will. I'll be there first thing." Ben looked around his office. Nothing seemed to be out of place, but he would do a more thorough check once he was allowed to clean up. "Do you have any idea why you think the clinic was targeted?"

Will shook his head before crossing his arms. "At this point, I don't. I can speculate, but that won't do either of us any good. The next step is for my guys to review the footage and go from there. Hopefully, by the time you come into the station, we'll have more information for you."

"Thank you." Ben sighed, still trying to make sense of everything that had happened.

"Do you have any plywood that we can board the window up with?"

Ben hadn't thought of that. Maybe at home, sure, but here, no. He wouldn't have anything.

"I'm gonna call a friend to see if he'll be able to bring some by." He pulled out his phone.

Will uncrossed his arms with a nod. "I'm going to step outside while you make the call. I want to inform my team about the footage. Try not to touch anything on your way out, at least until the crime scene analysts are done."

"Can I take care of the animals?"

"If they can wait another hour or so I'd leave them in the cages. If anyone of them needs attention by all means, though. Once my team is done, you're free to do whatever it is you need to do."

This was freaking wonderful. Ben's head started to pound as he watched Will stand in front of his office door.

First things first.

Ben quickly called John.

"*The only reason you should be calling me right now is 'cause you broke a tooth and are bleeding so much out of your mouth it looks like you got into a cage fight—*"

"Did anyone ever tell you that you're charming?"

"*All the time. What's got you calling me this late at night? Wait, did Holly try to cook?*"

Ben rubbed his hand on his forehead, trying to ward off his headache. "No, the house isn't on fire." He had to chuckle. It was their favorite joke between the two of them now. Holly didn't like it, but hell, it gave them a good laugh. He took a deep breath. "If only it were that easy. John, someone broke into the clinic tonight."

"*Holy shit. You're kidding?*"

Ben heard John rustling around. "I wish I was." He closed his eyes, trying to take a calming breath. "I need your help, can you do me a favor? I don't know if you'd have any at your house, but we need some plywood to board up the smashed front window until I can get a hold of the insurance company and figure out what we need to do. If you don't have any can you swing by my house? I've got some in the garage." Ben thought back to the large window up front. "We're gonna need a few pieces."

"Of course, man. I'm on my way."

"Thanks." Ben placed his phone in his back pocket before making his way out to the lobby of the clinic.

That's when he saw Holly standing in the middle of the room in handcuffs with Officer Jones holding onto one of her arms.

The second Holly spotted him, her eyes widened. "It's not what it looks like!"

Chapter Five

BY THE TIME everything at the clinic was back in order and there board over the broken window, it was well into the morning. Ben wasn't surprised at how long it took, he was just thankful it was done.

Ben scratched his head as he tried to make sense of the events that had transpired. He still couldn't wrap his mind around the clinic being broken into, especially since nothing ended up missing. All the medicines were accounted for, and even their petty cash was still there.

So then why would someone break in? It made no sense.

He looked around the room and spotted John moving one of the tables to its proper place. He'd never been more thankful for his best friend than he was right then. Without even a question, John arrived at the clinic and got to work. With John's help, everything was looking back to normal, minus the window.

Ben moved his attention toward the back room. While he and John worked on the cleanup, Holly stayed in the back making sure the animals were okay. That was a task on its own. The animals had no idea what was going on and to them the world was ending. Holly definitely had her hands full. And when you throw in all the loud noises from him and John, it was a recipe for disaster.

There was one thing that Ben knew for certain, though. He knew Holly had it covered. Her love for animals outweighed everything. There was no doubt in his mind Holly was able to take charge of the back while he and John did what they needed to do.

Although... Ben smiled. There was one mishap with a cocker spaniel that wanted out of the cage somewhere between one and two in the morning.

Holly might have had it handled, but there was never a moment *something* didn't go awry.

Thankfully, John was quick to grab the escaped convict as he came bouncing from the back room with a crazed Holly chasing after him.

Ben didn't know what was more entertaining: the dog purposely running back and forth in front of Holly taunting her, or Holly tripping on everything while cursing as she chased him.

It had definitely been a night.

"Thanks for helping," Ben remarked, looking at his best friend. "I owe you."

"Damn right you do." John looked over his shoulder at him as he moved the last chair in the waiting room into its proper place. "Are you going to call the insurance company and then get someone out here to fix the window?"

"That's the plan." Ben looked at his watch. It was six-forty-five. "They won't open for another hour, though."

"Good." John straightened before placing his hand on top of his stomach. He then puffed it out. "You have time to take me out for breakfast."

Ben's brow arched.

"What's with the pot belly?" Holly asked, coming from

the back staring at John sideways. Her scrunched face caused John to huff out a laugh causing his stomach to go back to normal. "Oh, that's more like it. Show those abs who's boss, big guy."

"Holly Richman," Ben growled at his wife, while giving her a pointed look.

"What?" Holly stared back at him. Her eyes sparkled with mischief. "He's got a nice tummy."

"And why are you looking at his *tummy?*" Ben asked tilting his head to the side.

"Hey, if you guys want to play your sports games without your shirts on, that's not my fault." Holly shrugged.

That little shit. He saw her bite her bottom lip to stop from laughing. *Oh, I'll give you something to laugh about. Just wait until tonight.*

Ben turned back to John, narrowing his eyes in warning. "From now on, you're wearing a shirt. End of story."

"Hey, don't go all asshole on me. It's not my fault your lady has good taste." John puffed out his chest. "I got the goods everyone wants a piece of." John started circling his hips.

"Eww!" Holly shuddered, throwing her hands over her eyes. "Don't ever do that again. I can't unsee it."

"Hey, you were all for my goods a few seconds ago." John pouted.

"No. I said you have a nice tummy." Holly moved in front of Ben before placing her hand on his abs. "But not as nice as his."

With a chuckle at John's flabbergasted expression, Ben bent and kissed the top of Holly's head. "Thank you, baby. But don't think I'll forget what you said."

"What? What did I say?"

Ben swatted her ass, causing Holly to jump. "If I ever catch you *staring* at John's goodies, there will be more of that to come."

"You can try, but you'd have to catch me first."

As Holly took a step away from him ready to run, Ben growled. *Oh, it's on.*

"For fuck's sake." John threw his hands in the air effectively distracting Ben from chasing his wife. "I'm right here. Can you all wait to do your kinky shit when I'm *not* around? Besides, let's get back to my *tummy* and feeding it." John pointed at Ben while looking at Holly. "Your husband just promised to take me out for a big breakfast. One that's going to make him question everything he knows with the amount of food I plan to consume."

"You have been known to pack it away. Where it goes, I have no idea. If I ate the way you do, I'd be as big as this room," Holly grumbled.

Ben sent a warning growl in her direction. *Oh, tonight is gonna be fun.*

Holly threw her hands up at his glare. "How about I stay here and start rescheduling patients? I'll call the clients who have animals here and tell them what happened. Sound good?"

Ben decided to drop the conversation about her talking bad about herself for later.... And there would be a later. "Sure. Do you have to go to work today?"

"Yes, but I'll call Mildred and let her know what's going on. She can cover for me until Stacy comes into the clinic. Actually..." Holly placed her finger on her chin. "When Stacy comes in, she can help me rearrange the appointments. Maybe I should tell Mildred I can't make it in. No wait, yes I can. It won't take long to do all this. If I remember correctly, you had a light day." She looked up at him. "Right, or am I making that up? Fridays are normally your off day. Maybe I'm losing my mind. Am I losing my mind?"

Ben couldn't help but laugh at her rambling. "Yes, babe. Fridays are normally my light day, and no you are not losing your mind. You just need some sleep." He leaned over and kissed her cheek.

"Sounds like she's got it under control," John chimed in. "Now, feed me."

"You're a pain in the ass." Ben looked at his best friend.

John straightened while he smirked. "Tis true."

"Fine." Ben rolled his eyes. *Is it too late to get a new best friend?* "But we're stopping at the station to file the report."

John's whole face brightened as a lopsided grin appeared. "You mean we're gonna do the walk of shame in and *out* of the police station?"

"Wait, what?" Holly asked.

"Yeah, what?" Ben mimicked.

"You know, only people with *stories* get to stroll out of the station doing the walk of shame." He pointed at his clothes before he placed both of his hands in his golden-brown hair and started disheveling it.

Holly and Ben both watched him in awe. "You're strange, you know that, right?"

"This is coming from the woman with a dog that thinks it's a human and that he's *your* master."

"Hey, you can't blame me for how my dog acts," Holly defended, as she placed her hands on her hips. "Have you ever tried to reason with him? It doesn't work. Plus, you can't say anything when *you're* the one trying to make yourself look like a crazy person so people will notice you and think you have some epic story to tell. And you say *me* having a human dog is strange."

"You enable him," John countered.

"Enabling him is safer. When Waffles eventually takes over the world I hope to get one of the better jobs." She pointed at

John. "You, on the other hand, will probably get pooper-scooper duty."

"And Ben will be imprisoned since he's a vet." John tsked at him. "No dogs like the vet."

Holly shrugged and looked at Ben. "He has a point."

"You know what? Both of you are strange." Ben scratched his chin. *But that does remind me to give Waffles a few extra treats when we get him from Henry's.*

John moved his hands through his hair one more time, causing Ben to roll his eyes.

"Let John do whatever the hell John's brain thinks is a good idea, Ben." Holly placed her hands in her pockets, looking away from him. "Plus, it's best you take him with you to the station anyway. I don't think it'd be wise for me to show my face there." Not looking at him, Holly started moving toward the reception desk, causing him to quirk his brow.

John burst into laughter. "What are you scared you'll run into Officer Jones?"

"He started it." Holly snapped her head toward John as her eyes narrowed on him.

"Holly." Ben gave her the eye.

"Do not Holly me, Ben! Jonsey boy had it out for me from the second we arrived." She crossed her arms over her chest. "He's a jerk face McJerkerson."

"You threatened him." Ben's brows shot to the ceiling.

"Is that why she was in cuffs when I got here?" John asked.

"No." Ben shook his head. "She was in cuffs because he ran her name and saw she'd been arrested before. Add in her threats and he said he did it for *safety* reasons."

John darted his eyes to Holly. "No shit. You've been arrested before?"

"It was a misunderstanding!"

"Just like last night was a misunderstanding? A misunderstanding that ended with you in handcuffs and me having to promise to keep you away from Officer Jones for the foreseeable future?"

"It's not my fault he can't handle me."

"He looked like he was handling you just fine. You were after all the one in cuffs. He was just standing there eating a donut." John laughed, which caused Holly to punch her fist in the air.

"That's another thing! He was taunting me with those donuts. Where the hell did they even come from?" she growled, narrowing her eyes at John. "You want a piece of me, Bub? Just say the word."

"Down girl." John held his hands up. "You're liable to trip on your way over here and break an arm."

Ben saw it coming from a mile away. You know that thing cats do right before they pounce? Apparently, Holly was part cat. He saw her take a small step back then shake her ass before she leaped into the air, her sights set on the man who was now hunched over uncontrollably laughing.

Thankfully, Ben caught her in mid-flight before cradling her in his arms. He kissed the top of her head. "Have I ever told you that you're sexy when you get all protective and domineering?"

John gagged. "Eww, not again."

Holly's face glowed as her eyes brightened. "Love you, Ben."

"Love you too, Grace." Ben placed a stray piece of Holly's hair behind her ear after setting her down. "I'll call you as soon as I'm done at the police station. See if Mildred wouldn't mind covering your whole shift so you can go home and get some sleep."

"What about you?"

"What about me?"

Holly looked at him. "You've been up as long as I have." The love and caring that radiated off Holly filled Ben with warmth. Her concern for everyone else was one of the biggest reasons why he loved her. Ben bent before kissing her lightly on the cheek. "Don't you worry about me. I'll be home before you know it and we can both take a nap."

"Does anyone care about me?" John whined. "I've been here just as long as you two. Don't I get a nap?"

Ben laughed before shaking his head at his friend. "You are pretty cranky."

"And hungry." John lifted his chin.

"Whoa." Holly looked at John. "You clearly *do* need a nap. You're on the brink of a temper tantrum like a two-year-old." Holly then turned and winked at Ben. "But that's someone else's problem, not mine."

Ben groaned at the realization.

"Right through the heart." John held his hand to his chest like he'd been shot. "And all this time I thought we had something going, Holly. I'm heartbroken."

Holly shrugged, before walking to the reception desk, leaving Ben to deal with John. "You'll get over it."

Chapter Six

AFTER SPENDING the morning rearranging all of Ben's appointments for the day, Holly was downright exhausted. Once Ben's receptionist, Stacy, made it in, they worked nonstop, which was a chore on it's own since Stacy nearly had a full-on meltdown once Holly told her what happened.

Thankfully, all of the clients had been very understanding, and there weren't any emergencies.

Holly closed her eyes the moment she pulled into her driveway.

Universe, when I asked for something interesting to happen for book material this was not *what I meant.* She finally let the events of the last twenty-four hours really sink in. *Holy freakin' crap on a cracker!*

No matter how hard she tried, she couldn't fathom any reason why someone would want to break into the clinic. Not only that, but *nothing* was taken.

It was like they only did it just to be a jerk.

Holly placed her hands on her forehead trying to ward off the headache she had.

Wonderful. As if today couldn't get any worse. She glared up at the roof of her car. *Now you're gonna give me a headache?*

Holly placed her head on the steering wheel. Well, it could have been worse. At least she didn't have to go to work.

Once Holly called Mildred and told her what happened, she was more than happy to cover for her.

Although Holly got the feeling if it were up to Mildred, she would have stormed into the police station demanding answers herself. Holly listened to Mildred for twenty minutes as she detailed what she'd do to the person who dared to hurt her *Mr. Hotness.* She was so up in arms, she was about five seconds from interrogating everyone she came across. Young or old, she didn't care.

Holly shuddered.

Calm and collected Mildred was a freaking tornado. Angry and determined Mildred was someone the freaking devil feared himself.

Me too, Holly thought as she smiled at Mildred's nonsense words when she started naming off her contacts and who she could call to *take care of it.*

Holly wouldn't be surprised if Mildred was at the library right now scouring through investigation books and crime dramas.

With a shake of her head, Holly pushed the thoughts of Mildred out of her mind and she reached for her phone. She hadn't heard anything from Ben. She really wasn't all that surprised though. She'd seen the way John ate before. If Ben were lucky, he would have gotten John out of the diner with only two meals instead of four. That man could eat everything in a buffet and *still* ask for more. Worst part was, he never gained a pound. He was still built like a damn cover model no matter what he stuffed in his large mouth.

Bastard.

They were probably just now getting to the station. Plus,

once they were at the police station, there was no telling how long they'd be there. The one and only time she had been arrested, she was there forever and a year.

She just hoped once this was all said and done, they'd never have to deal with it again.

Holly turned off her car and grabbed her bag. In slow movements, she dragged herself to the front door. Something was missing though. Once she made it up the last step, she realized it was quiet. Too quiet.

It was weird walking up to their house and not hearing barking.

Extremely weird.

She didn't like it.

Right before Holly left the clinic, she'd called her dad to give him the full rundown of the events that had transpired. After getting an earful from him too, Holly couldn't tell who was more pissed, her dad or Mildred.

Thankfully her dad agreed to watch the pups while she and Ben dealt with the situation.

It was a win-win. Henry always loved having the dogs around. He always spouted stuff about how the dogs made him young again and if we were only going to give him dogs and no grandbabies, then he'd take every moment he got with them.

Speaking of that...

Right now, she was too tired to really think about it. All she wanted was to crawl into their bed and never get back out again.

That wasn't too much to ask for, right? She didn't think so.

Holly opened the front door. When she looked down the hall, she saw Twitch running with all his might straight toward her. Her smile spread from ear to ear. *What a way to come home.* "Hey, little guy. Did you miss your momma?"

Twitch jumped on her legs, trying to get Holly to pick him up. She couldn't help but laugh as she reached down and scooped him into her arms. "You'd think I'd be used to you acting like a dog when we come home, don't cha?" She kissed his head. "But, I'm not."

When Ripley and Waffles were at the door ready to greet whoever was coming in, Twitch was always there too.

While Holly pat his head, she felt his little twitch, and her heart warmed. It wasn't as strong as it was when he was first poisoned, but it was still there. She suspected it would always be there. Especially since he'd grown out of his kitten phase and there was no sign of the twitch going away. But that was okay. It gave him character.

It made her love him all the more.

Holly scratched between his ears as she cooed at him. "How could anyone try to hurt you? You're nothing but a big lump of love."

Holly was just glad the kid who poisoned him had gotten in trouble. She still wanted to punch him whenever she thought about it, though.

But no, two wrongs don't make a right. And there was that whole being an adult thing and never punching a child. But still, anyone that hurts an animal and—

She stopped herself. Whenever she started going down that path it was never a good thing. And right now, she didn't have the energy.

She gave Twitch another squeeze. "Love you, Twitchy." She was rewarded when he started to rub against her chin while he purred.

Holly placed him on the floor before making her way toward their couch. With a dramatic sigh that could rival Lord Waffles, she plopped down.

Twitch was having none of it though. How dare his mom

get on the couch without him? He jumped onto her lap demanding more attention.

"My bad, sorry little one." Holly scratched under his chin before Twitch crawled into a ball.

A broad smile spread across Holly's face.

Ignoring her kitty, she reached into her pocket before pulling out her phone once again.

Nothing.

Holly let her eyes close. What a day it had been.

But even with everything that had happened, she still had one thing in the back of her head.

Holly knew there was no way she'd be able to bring up the conversation with Ben now. She'd been seconds from letting Ben know at dinner last night, but now it didn't seem the time nor place to bring it up. At least not today. Not while everything was still happening.

A longing ran through her body as her heart squeezed.

Soon.

Holly opened her eyes and looked around their home. "One day. One day it will happen." She let out a drawn-out sigh as she looked down at her lap. In an instant, she scooped Twitch into her arms before rolling onto her side. She brought her fur-baby up to her chin and carefully placed him in the crook of her neck. *This will have to do for now.*

Twitch opened one of his eyes briefly before stretching and making himself more comfortable.

"Glad to see I wasn't an inconvenience for you there, little mister."

Twitch yawned before shutting his eyes, completely ignoring Holly.

I can't tell if he missed me or he was just upset he was home alone this whole time and away from Ripley? She decided she would leave well enough alone. Ignorance is bliss as they say. At least he didn't talk back to her like Waffles did.

Yet.

HOLY SHIT, John can eat a lot.

Ben stared at his best friend in awe. *And how the hell was he able to run up these damn steps?*

"What's that look for?" John asked, as he took the steps two by two up to the front of the station.

"I'm trying to figure out how you're not over in the bushes spewing your breakfast. How the hell can you run after all the shit you just ate?"

John's face morphed into a boyish grin as he patted his stomach. "It's truly a gift."

"I can see that." Ben shook his head before also taking the steps two by two getting to the front of the station. *If John can do it. I can do it too. Hell, I'll take them three at a time.* "Promise me you won't do anything stupid."

"Like what?" John pushed his hair one more time.

Like that.

Ben strode past him, rolling his eyes. When he got to the front of the station he opened the door. To his surprise he saw one of his clients, Bruce's owner, sitting at the reception desk.

"Doctor Richman," she announced as she stood, throwing her hand out to shake his. "It's good to see you out of the clinic."

"Likewise," he replied a little taken aback to see her.

"When I came in this morning I heard some of the officers talking about what happened. I was going to call to see if you needed anything."

"That's very sweet of you..." Ben was at a loss for what to call her. Normally, he had a chart in front of him. Plus, he always categorized his clients by their pet's names.

"Please, call me Emma."

Ben gave her a small smile. "Thanks, Emma. How's Bruce?"

"He's fine. He's a big lug like usual."

Ben chuckled. That was right, other than Waffles tormenting him, Bruce was a giant teddy bear.

"Who's Bruce?" John asked as he made his way next to Ben.

"Oh, I didn't see you there." Emma turned toward John, her cheeks slightly colored.

John looked around the *empty* reception area and then back to them. "What do you mean you didn't see me? It's just us here."

Emma's face completely colored before she looked down at her hands in embarrassment. "Sorry," she whispered.

"Jackass." Ben punched John in the arm. *Idiot.*

"What? It was a valid question."

Emma looked at him with panic in her eyes. "I didn't mean anything by it. It's just when I saw Doctor Richman I kinda lost track of everything else. I've been in a panic about the break-in. It's such a wonderful establishment. I went to three other veterinarians before I found Doctor Richman and every other one looked at Bruce and wanted nothing to do with a scaredy dog who had issues. Or they wanted to put him on weird meds and I don't want that. Doctor Richman saw Bruce as he is. Perfect. Just a little broken. But that's okay because I'm a little broken too and that makes us perfect together." Ben saw Emma's eyes widen in horror as she realized she'd just word vomited—as Holly liked to call it—all over them.

Thankfully, he was used to Holly word vomiting most of the time, so he never changed his expression at Emma's confession. However, from the corner of his eye, he saw John take a step back.

If he says anything I swear to everything I'll murder him. Police station or no police station.

After a few seconds, John broke the silence. "It's okay, Ben does take up half the room."

"Are you jealous I have more muscles than you?" Ben narrowed his eyes at John as his lips thinned. His attention fully turned on him.

"You've got nothing compared to me. Who could be jealous of you?" John crossed his arms over his chest as he did his best to make himself look bigger.

"Obviously, you."

"Yeah right. How could I be jealous of you when I have this?" He pulled up his shirt showing his abs.

"Jesus Christ, no one wants to see that, you dimwit." Ben faked a gag.

However, when he heard a small laugh come from Emma he understood what John was doing. When Ben looked back at her, he could physically see her relief.

"I'm telling Holly." John glared at him.

"And what exactly are you going to tell my wife?" Ben arched his brow.

"I'm going to inform her *you* called *me* a name." John lifted his chin.

"What are you five?"

"No, I'm thirty-five. That's thirty more than five."

"I'm so glad you can count." Ben folded his arms across his chest. "Now if we can only get you to practice your manners, we'd be all set. Maybe we can move you out of pre-school."

"Now I'm telling her you said I had no manners." John's face morphed into shock.

"Emma," Ben turned to her, ignoring John. "Can you put me out of my misery and tell me where Detective Will Bower's office is?" He looked back at John. "The sooner I can get this over with, the sooner I can get rid of him."

"I'm your ride!"

"Don't remind me."

Emma shyly took another glance at John before looking back at Ben. "Is he always this dramatic?"

"Pretty much. I can never tell who's worse, him or Waffles."

"Oh." Emma's face brightened. "That little Corgi?"

"I don't know about *little*," John grumbled.

Ben shot his eyes back to John. "I'm telling Holly you said that."

"You wouldn't." John's eyes widened in horror.

"Try me."

Before John could retaliate, Emma chimed in. "Detective Bower is down the hall on the left. You can't miss him. I'll send him a quick message to let him know you're coming."

"Thank you." Ben gave her a small nod before walking around the reception desk, leaving John behind.

"Hey wait up, dickwad."

Ben sighed. *Give me strength.*

"Who was that?" John asked as he ran to catch up to Ben.

"She's a client. Couldn't you tell?"

"I figured as much." John looked over his shoulder back at the reception desk once more. "She's pretty. Kinda reminds me of Holly."

Ben stopped before pivoting to look at John. "What? Can I not say Holly's pretty? Is that against the bro code? It's not like I said she's fuckable or something. I mean she is, but all I said was she's pretty."

Ben cocked his brow. "Excuse me?"

John bounced his head back and forth. "You know what I'm saying. Holly's fuckable. I mean obviously you thought so." At Ben's deep growl John raised his hands. "Whoa, there, killer. Not that I ever thought anything of it. She's got a wack-a-doo dog and can't seem to figure out how to walk in a straight line without tripping. No one wants that kind of baggage. Plus, it's a compliment. One you are clearly not seeing."

"Explain to me why you saying my *wife* is fuckable is a compliment."

"It is," John protested. "I mean you do her, so obviously you agree. Or you wouldn't have married her."

"You know if we weren't surrounded by police officers I'd kill you where you stand, right?"

"You couldn't hurt a fly." John looked around the room, clearly glad they *were* surrounded by people in uniform. "Anyway, I was complimenting your client. She's pretty."

"So you said." *Pick your battles,* as his dad used to say.

Ben decided the best course of action was to ignore John. If he didn't, he most likely would be thrown in jail.

Turning back, he looked down the hall. That's when he spotted Officer Jones. "Hey, it's good to see you again," Ben announced as he made his way toward him. "Arrest anyone interesting?"

"Other than your wife?" John said, coming up from behind him.

"He didn't arrest her," Ben spat, glaring at his dimwitted best friend. "He only detained her for a few minutes."

"Oh yes, the curvy woman with a loud mouth." Officer Jones took a drink from the mug he was carrying.

"That would be her." Ben nodded with a smirk.

Officer Jones looked behind them. "Is she by chance with you?"

Ben watched as the officer's left hand went to the handcuffs on his belt.

"No," he said, looking back at John with wide eyes.

"Pity."

"Jones, stop being an ass." Will made his way out of a nearby office. "Ignore him, please. He finds it *fun* to intimidate people. Your wife turned out to be the perfect person for Jones to, excuse my lack of a better term, but *fuck* with."

Jones shrugged, not denying it. Ben could see the hint of a smile on Jones's face. That's when Ben's body relaxed. "She is a fun one to rile, isn't she?"

A ridiculously wide smile spread across Officer Jones's face before walking away.

"What just happened?" John asked.

"I think he likes to mess with people and Holly just became his prime target."

"And how do you feel about that?"

Ben shrugged. "It might be fun to watch."

John's face brightened in pure amusement as he gave that all-knowing look. "Can I watch too?"

Ben tried but failed to hide his smile as he brought his attention back to Will. As long as Officer Jones didn't actually do anything to harm or scare Holly, he'd be all for a little harmless prank or two. Maybe he could talk to Officer Jones on the way out.

Plus, being able to rescue Holly out of the situation last night sent a wave of *white knight* through Ben.

Yeah, I'm definitely going to talk to Officer Jones before we leave.

"Let's go into my office so we can get this paperwork finished," Will announced before leading Ben and John into his office.

BEN WALKED into the house to see Holly curled up with Twitch on the couch. At the sight, he warmed. They looked picture perfect together.

Even after the craziness of the last twenty-four hours, Holly still looked downright beautiful. Her hair was all over the place and her mouth was just the tiniest bit open as she slept.

She was fucking breathtaking and he knew it. His eyes traced along the curve of her body as he took her in.

He was a lucky bastard and he knew it.

He had to bite back his groan as his dick pressed against the front of his pants. It took all of his willpower to control himself.

She looked so peaceful as she slept. Plus, Ben knew she needed it. So did he. And if that meant a case of blue balls then so be it.

Her body did look inviting though. As he scanned her sleeping form one more time, his eyes focused on Twitch. He was curled tightly under Holly's chin. As if the little guy could sense Ben staring at him, he opened one eye. He gave Ben a quick once-over before closing his eyes again, promptly dismissing him.

Good to know who you like better there, Bub. Ben could swear he saw Twitch open his eyes and then roll them. *I'll remember this come shot time.*

He was definitely going to have to start separating Waffles from the rest of the gang every once in a while.

Looking back at Holly, he decided to sneak in behind her and curling up was a much better plan than going into their bed alone.

As quietly as he could, he removed his shoes and socks along with his shirt. He eyed his delectable wife. One of his favorite things was to cradle her to his body as they slept. Although, halfway through the night, it never failed. Holly would threaten him with death if he didn't move over and give her some space. She'd mumble how between him, Waffles, Ripley, and now Twitch she'd end up dying of heat stroke.

Only Holly.

He knew if he was careful, he'd be able to finagle his way behind Holly and nap with her in his arms.

And that was exactly what he was going to do.

Ben tiptoed over to the couch before placing his left leg behind Holly's knees. Before he made his next move, he glanced at her to make sure he hadn't woken her.

Okay, now what?

Seeing as she was still asleep, he started maneuvering himself behind Holly. When he was halfway in place, he saw Twitch turn his head to stare at him like he was crazy.

Ben narrowed his eyes right back at him. *You know, instead of judging me you could help.*

Twitch closed both of his eyes before stretching out getting more comfortable.

Figures.

Ben carefully bent his knee, placing his full weight onto the back of the couch.

See this wasn't so hard. Alright, now just wedge yourself between the couch and Holly.

He was making damn good progress if you asked him. He was nearly fully wedged where he wanted to be when he heard a tiny laugh escape from his wife.

"You're awake, aren't you?"

"I plead the fifth."

Ben growled before bumping Holly with his hips, giving him the room he needed. "You could have just moved over, you know?"

"And miss out on this acrobatic feat? No way." She turned her upper body to face him with a huge grin.

That little shit.

"You think you're funny, don't you?" He tried his best to give her a stern look, but failed miserably.

"Maaayyybbbeee," she cooed before scooting to the front of the couch giving him all the room he needed.

"You're gonna get it, Grace."

"You keep telling yourself that, honey." Holly patted his side.

"Oh, Mrs. Holly Richman," he growled in her ear. "I think you know damn well what I can do to you." He pushed his hips forward causing his dick to rub against her ass.

Holly let out a tiny gasp before she wiggled her hips back into his groin. "Oh, do tell. I'm always in the mood to be enlightened."

Ben pushed her hair from her neck before nibbling on the exposed skin. "I thought you were tired."

"Not anymore." She turned to face him giving complete access to her mouth, which he gladly took.

Fuck yes.

He ground his hips into her as he devoured her mouth. With his free hand, he reached around her body and grabbed onto her breast, enticing a moan from her.

Fuck, he loved his wife. He loved every fucking inch of her.

Without removing his lips from hers, he inched his hands lower. Once he found the hem of her shirt, he snaked his hand under it. Her skin was so heated it sent his blood racing. Right now, his dick was pressed so forcefully to his pants he was sure there'd be a permanent zipper mark.

He didn't give a shit though. His hand moved up her belly seeking out her taut peaks.

"Ben," Holly whispered, pulling her mouth from his.

Ignoring her cries, he sought out her mouth again.

He was instantly rewarded when her hand moved between their bodies and started to palm his member through his jeans. "Fuck," he growled, as shivers moved down his spine.

"What do you think I'm trying to do?" Her words ignited him. Quickly he moved his hand to his belt undoing it with ease. As soon as there was room, Holly shoved her hand inside his pants seeking out his dick. The second she reached the base, he couldn't stop himself from thrusting his hips forward.

"You're awful happy to see me." Holly smirked at him as her hand stroked up and down his dick.

"I'm always happy to see you." Ben didn't know if it was all the excitement of the recent events or that this was just how crazy his wife normally made him, but he *had* to be inside of her. If he didn't, he'd die.

There was something about Holly's warm body next to his that fucking sent him into hyper-drive.

As Holly worked him, he reached around her waist once again cupping her sex. The heat he felt through her leggings almost fucking unmanned him.

He moved his hand to her waistband. Thank fucking God she had on leggings. He easily pushed his hand past the material.

The moment his fingers brushed against her lower lips, Holly gasped throwing her head back.

Fuck he loved this.

He let his fingers slide against her slowly, teasing her, causing Holly to start to thrash around. "No teasing, more doing!"

At her words, he bit down onto her neck. He placed his index and middle finger at her entrance. "Please," she begged.

He pushed his fingers deep inside her. She shot her hips off the couch.

He fucking loved watching her like this.

Holly, the equal opportunist she was, used her hot little hand and grabbed onto his dick before giving a squeeze. "More," she panted.

If Holly wanted more, well he was damn well going to give it to her. He hoped like hell these were not her favorite leggings.

Fuck it, I'll buy her more.

He sat up, pulling his hand from her center.

"No!"

He ignored Holly's cry as he flipped her over onto her stomach. He then grabbed a hold of her leggings at her ass and ripped them in half exposing her perfect bottom.

"I'm gonna murder you for that." She looked over her shoulder at him. *Ehh, it was worth it.* Plus, he would have been more concerned if he didn't see lust staring back at him. Not to mention the fact she kept pushing her ass into the air.

"I'll remind you to murder me later. Right now, I'm busy." He bent kissing her exposed flesh before biting it.

Holly pushed her ass back at him. It was a sight to worship.

He palmed her ass before seeking out her core with his tongue. He took one long lick as he moaned. Fuck, even after all this time she still tasted like pure fucking honey. He could eat her all day and still not tire.

That's it, he had to be inside her. The thing about relationships was, sometimes you needed slow-burning sex. Other times you needed to fuck. Smart men knew the difference.

Holly moaned as he worked her. Ben pulled back before he grabbed onto her leggings and ripped them near in half now.

"I'm gonna kill you!" she shouted, looking over her shoulder at him. When she saw his smirk she sent him a dirty look.

"They were already ruined, Grace." He ignored her as he moved his hands to his pants. He grabbed a hold of his dick finally freeing it. He looked down at her pussy, and his mouth watered. Her lush lips were swollen and coated in her cream. He couldn't help but palm himself at the site.

When she shook her ass, he lost all control.

He lined up and entered her in one quick move.

GOD HOLLY LOVED it when Ben got like this, and right now this was exactly what they needed. Especially after all the stress of the break-in.

The moment he was fully inside of her everything felt right again.

Then she felt it. "Ouch."

Ben stopped his movements. That's when it happened again. "Owie."

"What's going on?" Holly heard the concern in Ben's voice, before she could say anything she felt it again. When she looked over her shoulder, she saw Twitch's orange and white head bobbing up and down. *What the hell?*

Twitch then did what Twitch did best. He reared back and jumped to the side of her leg, his claws out for attack.

Ben barked out a deep laugh. "Holy shit, he's playing with your ripped leggings."

Holly felt a pull on the material and sure enough, Twitch had a piece of it in his mouth and was pulling with all his might.

"Stop it." Holly reached for the torn piece only to have her hand swatted away by Twitch's paw. When she tried to grab it again Twitch growled at her. A full-on angry cat, *this is my prize, kind of growl.*

She glanced back at Ben who was in full hysterics at his point. "Help me!"

Ben held onto his stomach as he laughed. "I'm trying."

"No, you're not!" Holly reached for the fabric again but was once again warded off. "Ouch. Twitch you don't do that to your momma! You're going in time out!" Holly pushed onto her forearms. *I swear to all things, if it's not one animal it's the next.*

"Don't you dare move," Ben demanded.

Amongst his laughter he grabbed onto the part of her leggings and ripped it clean off. "Ben!"

"What?" He cocked his brow at her. Ben took the ruined fabric and chucked it across the room, which had a crazed Twitch run full speed after it.

"That'll take care of him." He bent to her back ready to kiss it. Unfortunately, Twitch had other ideas. With his prize in his mouth he came back running to Ben.

Twitch dropped it at his foot.

"You have got to be fucking kidding me," Ben growled. "Does he want me to play fetch with him?"

Holly watched the scene in astonishment. When Twitch picked up the piece of fabric and then dropped it at Ben's foot again she lost it. "Holy crap, he's doing what Ripley does when you play fetch with her."

When Holly pushed herself back, her core brush against Ben, causing a shiver to run through her. Oh man, she was so torn. Should she deal with her crazy cat or continue what they were doing?

Damn it.

"Twitchy." Ben did his best to handle the situation. He picked up the piece of fabric and balled it into his hands. "Hey little guy, you want this?" Twitch jumped and eyed the material. "Nope. How about I throw this and you go find Ripley. Go show her what you found. You know she'll love it."

Ben tossed the fabric in the middle of the floor. Holly's mouth fell open the moment Twitch ran after it and then pranced out of the room with the legging piece in his mouth.

"Holy hell, is he really going to look for her?" Her eyes widened.

"Fuck, if I know." Ben laughed, before turning his attention back to her. "That just means we have no time to lose." Ben placed his fingers at her core and started massaging her again. Instantly, a new wave of heat flowed through her.

God, how can he do that so fast? She looked over her shoulder at him, he was once again stroking himself. Her insides clenched. Watching him touch himself always sent her over the edge.

"You ready for me, Grace?"

She pushed her hips back answering him. "Put it in me," she demanded. "And you better hurry before Twitch remembers Ripley isn't here." Holly wiggled her hips demanding for him to move. Ben grabbed her hips and slowly entered her again.

Ben pulled out, only leaving the tip.

She snapped her head over her shoulder to give him a

warning look. *Not today, Bub. I know what I want.* She slammed her hips back causing him to enter her. "Fuck me," he growled. Ben tightened his grip on her hips as he started to move inside of her.

As they found their frantic rhythm, Holly could feel herself building.

"Harder." Holly pushed herself onto her hands before bouncing back on him with force.

Something must have snapped in Ben. He placed both of his hands on her shoulders pushing himself harder inside of her.

"Yes!" Holly screamed as she started to feel her body quiver.

Ben grabbed her middle lifting her as he fell onto his side. He then placed her right leg over his hip as he continued his thrust.

Holly could feel every one of her nerve endings. She loved this position. Ben snaked his hand around her body seeking out her clit. Once he found it he started rubbing in circles.

"Oh, I'm gonna-I'm gonna," Holly panted as she met him thrust for thrust. She was right there. When Ben pinched her clit, she exploded. Through her ecstasy Ben grabbed her hips and started moving faster, then with a loud groan, he bit down onto her neck as he came deep inside her.

Holy crap on all the crackers.

They both laid there panting as they tried to get their breathing back under control.

Ben slowly kissed along her neck before he pushed himself onto his elbow to kiss her lips.

"Well, if I knew you were gonna do that when you got home I would have never taken a nap."

Ben huffed out a laugh as he placed the palm of her hand onto her belly. "Like you didn't know this was gonna happen?

You planned it." He gave her a pointed look. "I came home and there you were, sexy as hell spread out on the couch. You knew what you were doing." He sent her a quick wink before kissing her neck.

"So, you're saying I'm just so sexy all I have to do to get you turned on is drool and snore a little?"

"Oh, Grace, that's the shit that gets me hard for days," he laughed, gently biting down on her earlobe. "Those snores." She heard a growl escape from him.

Holly started to laugh but then quickly stopped. "Hey, hey, no more groping for you. I'm mad at you." She narrowed her eyes. "As soon as I regain some strength I'm kicking your ass for destroying my favorite pair of leggings."

Ben's face morphed into a lazy grin. "If I didn't destroy them would I have been able to do this?" He slowly pushed himself inside of her again.

"Mmhmm." Holly's eyes started to roll back in her head before she snapped them open. "No. Stop trying to distract me. You didn't have to go all Neanderthal on them, you could've just pulled them down. And now a piece of them is a freaking chew toy for Twitch."

"Could of, would of, should of." He shrugged.

Holly's face broke into a smile. "Do you think we lose points for us still being pretty much dressed?"

"Mistakes were made." Ben's grin spread from ear to ear. "Love you, Grace."

"Love you too, Ben." Holly's eyes started to close. That's when she felt something land on her. When she opened her eyes, she was greeted by an evil glare coming from Twitch. "I wasn't the one that lied to you."

Ben moved his hand to scratch Twitch behind the ears. "Your mommy's a mean old liar, isn't she?"

Holly snapped her eyes to Ben with a glare. "I'm the liar?"

"Shh." Ben ignored her. "Can't you tell Twitch wants to take a nap?" He pulled Holly into his arms.

"I'm going to remember this. Both of you!"

"Sleep." Ben chuckled as he made himself comfortable.

Holly crossed her arms over her chest pushing Twitch to lay on Ben. "Don't tell me what to do!"

Chapter Eight

IT HAD BEEN a total of three weeks since the break-in. Three freaking weeks and they were still no closer to getting any answers than they were on day one. Holly didn't know whether to pull her hair out or cry.

And poor Ben.

Her heart broke for him. He'd been so stressed about the whole situation. And add in the insurance company dragging their feet, having no idea if they'd be broken into again, and what you got was Ben as a full-blown mess.

Which in turn made her a mess.

Try as she might, Holly still hadn't been able to bring up the conversation about having a baby. Which added another weight to her shoulders.

There'd only been one time she thought she could broach the subject, and she really was seconds from doing just that.

Then to her utter shock, the moment she was ready to spill her guts, Ben started talking about how he wanted to add extra security to the clinic. But that wasn't the big, *what* moment. No, that came when he pulled out blueprints to add on a pseudo clinic onto the house so he could bring home all the animals that were left at the clinic overnight.

That was a shock.

Sure, she got where he was coming from. Ben would cut off his own arm if it meant keeping his animals out of harm's way. That was one of the many reasons she loved him. Ben's heart was huge and completely full of love.

So was hers.

But the idea of having a revolving door of boarded or sick patients at the house sounded like it would do more harm than good.

Talk about added stress.

She couldn't deny his heart was in the right place, though, but with everything going on he also wasn't thinking clearly. It wouldn't be smart to keep moving animals that were recovering back and forth every night.

Not to mention, Waffles would lose his shit.

Or worse...

He'd probably convert every single one of Ben's patients to overthrow the government and rule the world with him as their new leader.

Nobody needed that in their life. Plus, it was bad enough Ripley had picked up ninety-five percent of Waffles' traits by being around him. Holly didn't need Ben's clients calling her complaining about how their pets now acted.

Besides, could you imagine a whole hoard of *Lord Waffles* running around?

Holly shuddered.

Nope, a pseudo clinic on the house was not the answer.

Ben knew that, and so did she.

Regardless, that didn't stop Ben from constantly worrying about what could happen next.

Maybe they were just overreacting.

Holly was sure once everything was straightened out, all

would go back to normal. Well, at least she sure as hell hoped it would.

Especially for her.

Holly had been irritable and moody since everything happened. She kept chalking it up to a crappy sleep schedule, and the fact she hadn't found the time to talk to Ben, but still, her constant mood swings were starting to drive her up the wall.

Oh, and let's not forget her godforsaken heartburn. Shit, it was like her heart was a freaking volcano and every hour it had to erupt. Maybe it was the unhealthy amount of donuts she'd been consuming, or maybe it was all the stress.

Regardless of what the root cause was, she was sucking down antacids like they were her new favorite candy.

Speaking of which...

Holly opened her bottom desk drawer to retrieve her antacids. Her heartburn was in full swing this morning. At this point, she was about three seconds from deciding if she wanted to grind down the whole bottle of antacids and make a smoothie or fall into the fetal position and pray for sweet death.

She'd be lying if she didn't say she was leaning toward the latter.

"Do I need to call our Benny Boy and tell him he's lacking in the sack again?" Mildred asked as she walked into the room with a stack of books in her hands. She plopped them onto the papers Holly was going over.

Holly's eye started to twitch.

Universe, give me strength. Taking a deep breath, she arched her brow at the old coot. "Please tell me you do not call my husband and say crazy shit like that?" Holly stared at the person who, now that she thought about it, was probably the cause for her ungodly amount of heartburn and stress.

"Me and Benny have conversations all the time," Mildred

nonchalantly answered plopping her hip on the desk. "Sadly, he refuses to tell me about his man meat though." Her brows knitted together as she pouted.

"You're joking, right? Please tell me you're joking?"

"Do I ever joke about man sticks? I think not, missy. You do not joke about such things." The appalled expression on Mildred's face had Holly paling.

Universe, how is this my life? Am I your favorite sitcom to watch? That must be it. I'm primetime entertainment for you. That's the only *reason this conversation is happening right now.*

Mildred sighed. "Benny Boy normally thinks I'm joking. Pity." Mildred looked at Holly with a hurt expression. "What am I doing wrong?"

Oh, for the love of all things... Holly rolled her eyes. "I don't know, maybe it's the fact you're asking my husband about his... how did you put it, oh yes, *man stick*?" Holly threw her hands in the air with resignation. "You know what, I'm going to pretend we didn't have this conversation."

Although, as soon as she got home she was damn well going to ask Ben some questions. And he better have some answers.

"Fine, suit yourself." Mildred started foraging through the papers on Holly's desk. "Now, back to you. Why do you look like someone kicked your dog?"

Instead of answering her, Holly zoned in on Mildred rummaging through her stuff. "What are you doing?"

"Looking for donuts." She gave Holly a 'duh' look. "You have donuts on your desk every day."

"Maybe I don't have any today." Mildred's brows went to the ceiling. "Fine." Holly opened up her drawer and placed a box on the top of the desk. Holly threw her hand on top of the box glaring at Mildred stopping her. "Only one!"

"Yay." Mildred's grabby hands pushed Holly's out of the way before opening the box. "You must have one of those newfangled reward cards with the donut shop with how many times you go in there. You must be in the frequent flyers section by now."

"Don't remind me." Holly groaned. "I've already put on about eight pounds." She reached for the donuts. "I can't seem to stop. There is something about these things that I crave. If I don't have it, I feel like I'm going to die."

"That's not a healthy way to live there."

"Trust me, I know. But with everything going on, I can't seem to say no." Holly shrugged throwing another piece in her mouth.

"As long as you keep bringing them in, I don't really care. Now, where were we? That's right, you were about to spill your guts about the attitude you got going on." Mildred made a weird moan as she took a bite of her donut. "Momma needs some good gossip to bring back to my knitting club."

"You don't knit."

"Neither do they. We just sit around and gossip for a few hours each week." Mildred shoved the rest of the food into her mouth chomping happily on it. "You should have heard the stuff they were spouting when we were talking about Ben's nutty mother last year. Oh boy, you think *I'm* bad. You should have heard some of those ladies."

Holly shuddered as the thought tingled down her spine. "It's good to know my life is a constant source of entertainment to you and your *knitting* friends."

"You do keep it lively." Mildred smirked at her. "Now spill."

Holly slumped into her chair with a heavy sigh. "I don't know, Mildred. It's everything. Ben's worried about the clinic. Now he's talking about building a room onto the house to keep the animals overnight. The insurance company is a freaking joke. We haven't heard anything about the investigation. I can't write. At all..." Holly sent a death glare to Mildred when she reached into the box again. "And *you* keep eating my donuts."

Mildred shrugged before pulling out the last donut taking a bite. "So, you're saying life is hard and you're having a pity party?"

"Have I ever told you I want to murder you?"

"About once a day. If you didn't, I'd worry you don't love me anymore." Mildred straightened. "Now, let's work on this one step at a time. Ben wants to bring his patients home at night because he's afraid someone else might break into the clinic?"

"Yes, he's got it into this head it wasn't just a prank and it was someone after him or something. I kinda agree with him, though. Remember right after we got married Ben found out about all that stuff at Richman Industries after his mother left and the new board took over?"

"Oh yeah, the embezzlement. The ladies and I at knitting went to town on that one." Mildred nodded. "But I thought all of that had been handled and the new board of directors was doing well?"

"They are." Holly closed her eyes for a second. "Ben said something about one of the employees that were fired going after him. Especially, since he was the one that forced his mother to leave effectively destroying their coverups. So, he's now constantly worried about what is going to happen next."

"That doesn't sound like our Ben one bit." Mildred crossed her arms over her chest.

"Then for some reason the insurance company is being an asshat. Since nothing was taken, per the police report they're saying crap like they have to do their own *investigation*." Holly looked at her. "Can you believe they think we did it on purpose to file a claim? Have they lost their damn minds? Ben has enough money to fix a million windows. But no, we did it all just to get a few lousy dollars." She rolled her eyes. "Leave it to the insurance company to be a jackass."

"It'll get worked out. It always does."

Now that Holly had started, though, there was no stopping her. "You'd somehow think with Will being Ben's friend we would've heard something by now about the investigation, but no. Nothing. What's the use in having friends working on the case, if they can't even help you?"

Mildred nodded. "I told you. One phone call and I can have all of your problems taken care of. You don't get to live this long without meeting some *interesting* people."

Holly laughed. "Thanks, but no thanks. I don't think your type of help will keep us out of jail."

Mildred shrugged. "Suit yourself." Her lips scrunched together. "What I should really do is march my butt into the station and teach those officers about how to do their jobs."

Holly cocked her head to the side "Oh, I'm begging you, *please* enlighten me about why you think you could do a better job than them, or how you're qualified to?"

"Since the break-in I've spent night and day reading up on crime dramas. I'm pretty sure I could walk into that station and teach them all a thing or two. Hell, I bet if I started right now I could figure out exactly what happened and in *less* time." Mildred pulled out the pad and pen she kept in her skirt apron.

"What are you doing?"

"Writing down my evidence. Duh. What do you take me for, some rookie cop?"

"You're not a cop."

"The people I'm interrogating don't need to know that." She started scribbling stuff down.

"Mildred, please don't go around interrogating people. That's only going to add to my stress level and right now I don't think I can take that."

Mildred eyed her. "You do look a little flushed."

"Yeah, well that's probably 'cause you give me anxiety *and* this morning I woke up feeling like shit."

Mildred stared at her before nodding once.

"Really, that's all you've got for me? A nod. Normally, you'd be demanding I tell you all my symptoms. And then you'd be off in the medical section looking up my disease."

Mildred placed her pen at her mouth thinking. "Cop or doctor? Decisions, decisions."

Holly shook her head. "How about librarian?"

"Nah, that's boring."

"Yet it's what you've done your whole career."

"Exactly, so I need some more excitement in my life."

"No, no one needs you to have more excitement in your life. You're good."

Mildred sent her a look which Holly decided it was best to ignore her.

After a few uncomfortable minutes of Mildred staring her down, she sighed. "I'll stick with cop for the day."

"Glad you've made your decision."

"Besides, I don't need to play doctor I already know what's wrong with you."

Holly sat straighter in her chair lifting her right brow at the crazy old lady. "Oh, don't keep me in suspense. Please inform me what the oh so mighty Doctor Mildred has surmised by only creepily staring at me."

"Missy, I wouldn't be so quick to discount me." She reached for the donut Holly had been munching on, before she placed it on the stack of papers in front of her. The moment Holly saw what she was doing she lunged for it. "Mine."

Unfortunately for her, Mildred was pretty quick for an old lady.

"And right there proved it." Mildred shoved the last piece

into her mouth causing Holly's heartburn to come back in full force as she pictured all the ways she could murder her coworker.

"How is my trying to stop your grabby old hands from stealing my food proof of whatever the hell it is you think I have?"

Mildred shrugged again, which was sure as hell getting annoying.

Mildred pointed at her. "You're moody. Has anyone ever told you you're rude when you're moody? Little old ladies like me need all the food we can get. Especially, if I'm gonna be the detective that breaks the case. It's a stereotype of eating all the donuts. And, I *must* uphold it."

Give me strength, please universe I know you're sitting there laughing your ass off but please give me strength not to murder her. "So, I guess we're back to you being a cop?"

"I never stopped." She pulled out her pad and pen in her lap. "Now, let me ask you a question."

"I can't stop you." Holly sat back staring at her.

"That's right. You can't. You say you're stressed, right? You have bad heartburn all the time. Don't give me that look, there, young lady. I see you sucking down those antacids like they are going out of style. And you can't stop with these majestic goodies." She pointed to the donut box. "Although I cannot blame you on the last one."

"If I play along with your craziness, will you leave me alone to work on this paperwork?"

"I'd be lying if I said I would, but I'll make a deal with you."

"I'm all ears."

"I'm going to put away my Detective Mildred hat and put on my Doctor Mildred hat and ask you one question. If you can answer me with honesty, I will walk away for the rest of the shift and leave you to pout on your own."

Holly narrowed her eyes at her, while her lips thinned. "And who's to say I wouldn't answer you with honesty?"

"I'll know."

"Fine." Holly crossed her arms over her chest. "Lay it on me, Doctor Mildred. What's my diagnosis?"

"If you are going to huff at me, I'll take my expert knowledge and leave."

"Is that all I've ever had to do to get you to leave me alone?" Her brows shot to the ceiling.

"I take it back. I'll sit here all day and ask you about how Ben uses his ding-dong."

"Can we not," Holly groaned.

"Sure. The choice is yours. Now, answer me this, are you sure you don't already have a bun baking?"

"I don't cook. You know that."

Mildred rolled her eyes before she sighed. "You're a lost cause. I'm going to the true crime section. Holler if you need anything." With that Mildred hopped off the desk with her pen and pad in hand and started making her way to the crime section.

Crazy old woman. Why does she always have to talk in riddles and nonsense? Why can't she just come out and say whatever the hell she is trying to say?

Holly grabbed one of the books on her desk Mildred left and pulled out the inventory paper she'd been working on. "Stupid hag. Everyone knows I can't cook. And baking." She huffed. "The one and only time I tried it, I nearly set the kitchen on fire. With baking you have to be all precise and stuff, that's annoying. No one has time to read *every* step," she mumbled. "And to make bread... that sounds like hell. Plus, I wouldn't know the first thing about baking buns I would—"

She froze.

Are you sure you don't already have a bun baking?

Holly sat there in shock as Mildred's words finally took

hold. *Oh my God!* She tried to think about the last time she had her period.

"Oh shit."

Holly jumped from her seat and started making her way toward the front door. When she walked passed the crime section she hollered. "I've got to go, cover for me."

All Holly heard as she walked through the door was a giddy Mildred screaming, "Congratulations!"

Chapter Nine

BEN PLOPPED on the couch with a heavy sigh. No matter how much he tried to work things out with the insurance company, nothing he did seemed to work. Today he'd decided to take a half-day and come home early.

He wanted to look over his plans of possibly adding a room onto their house anyway. Sure, Holly didn't seem to be one hundred percent thrilled about the idea, but at this point what other choice did they have?

Other than Holly, Henry, and their own pets, his patients were his priority. And if that meant housing them at night then so be it. Plus, there was that sinking feeling he had about the break-in. Something wasn't right.

If it were just a prank, he'd know. This. This was different.

Ben didn't know *why* he felt that way, but he did.

And it was getting to him. Over the last few weeks, Ben found himself driving over to the clinic after he'd closed up for the night to make sure everything was fine.

It always was, but there was still an unsettled feeling inside of him.

What if it really was some of the fired employees of

Richman Industries had it out for him? Sure, some of them were sent to jail but the ones they couldn't prove beyond a reasonable doubt, were just fired. What if they now blamed him for their downfall. And taking it out on the clinic would be where it would hurt him most. Well, not the most. If anyone ever laid a finger on Holly, they'd be dead before they knew what was coming to them. Hell, he bet before he could do anything Mildred would have called in her goons to take care of them.

He sighed closing his eyes.

Maybe it was payback. Or, maybe it was just a prank.

He needed a vacation.

A real vacation.

Ben brought his hand to his forehead and started rubbing away his headache.

After he and Holly were married, they only went on a four-day honeymoon to a little cabin in the woods.

Shit, those were the best four days of his life. If it were up to him they would have *never* left. He didn't think they wore clothes the entire time they were there, which was fine by him. And if you ignored the time Holly fell out of the bed, hitting the nightstand with her knee and sending it crashing to smithereens onto the floor, there were no mishaps.

It was just him, his fucking gorgeous wife, and no clothes.

Perfection.

Unfortunately, reality had set in far too soon. Although he would have loved to stay there forever, he needed to get back to his patients and then there was Henry. They had made sure he'd have enough food and everything was in order, Holly nor Ben liked leaving him alone for too long.

Especially when he was watching the dogs. Originally John had agreed to watch them, even if that meant having to deal with Waffles and his judgmental side-eye. Henry was having none of that. And the second Henry took a page straight out of Waffles' book and gave Holly the sad puppy eyes, she couldn't say no.

At least he got John to take care of Twitch. Then again, keeping Twitch away from Ripley caused some issues for John. He still motions to the spot on his arm where Twitch scratched him.

Ehh, it was John. He needed a little defiance in his life.

Ben let his head fall back on the couch.

Damn, he needed a vacation.

Something nudged at his leg. When he opened his eyes he saw Waffles. "What can I do for you, your holiness?"

Waffles barked before looking toward the kitchen. "It's not dinnertime."

Waffles barked again causing Ben to arch his brow. "Does your mother feed you extra meals when's she's home?"

Waffles *and* Ripley barked in unison this time.

"She does now? Well, I'm gonna have to have a little talk with her." Ben slowly moved off the couch before trekking into the kitchen. "One treat. That's it. I'd say don't tell your mother I'm spoiling you two, but seeing as she feeds you extra meals, I'm pretty sure I still have the upper hand."

Ripley and Waffles both sat perfectly as they waited for their snacks. Ben tossed them each one before leaning against the counter.

Speaking of Holly...

Ben placed his chin in the palm of his hand. Something was off with her. He could sense it. He'd been meaning to talk to her about it, but with everything going on it never seemed like the right time. Plus, whenever they finally got a few minutes that weren't dedicated to something else... He jumped her. Ehh, what could he say? His wife was sexy. There was no shame in that.

Regardless though, something was off.

His brows drew together as he scratched the scruff on his

chin. She'd been a little snippy the past few weeks. Then this morning, before she left for work she'd mentioned how she wasn't feeling well. Her face did look flushed, and she now had antacids on every table in their house.

Maybe he should make her an appointment at the doctor? Yeah, that's exactly what he was going to do. Ben reached into his back pocket retrieving his phone. As he was about to make the call, though, he heard someone speed into their driveway.

He glanced at the time on his phone. There was no way Holly would be home already.

He made his way toward the front door to investigate with a barking Waffles and Ripley at his feet. The moment the door came into view he saw Holly throw open the door. She tripped over the frame landing on her hands and knees flinging the bag she was carrying in her hands across the room.

Instantly he ran to her side picking her up. "Grace, are you okay?"

Holly must not have registered that it was him since she jumped out of his arms and screamed before holding up her fists ready to fight.

It took everything in him not to burst into laughter.

Once she realized it was him, she held her hand to her chest as she tried to regain her breath. "Where in the hell did you come from?"

"The kitchen," he answered. "Are you okay, did you hurt yourself?"

Holly bent dusting off her pants. "Yeah, yeah I'm fine. Don't worry about me. Why are you home?" she asked in a panic.

When Ben really looked at her, he saw an urgency in her eyes he hadn't seen before, causing his brows to knit together. "I took a half day, Grace."

"Oh, okay good, good." Holly pushed her hair out of her face in panicked movements. "Wonderful. I mean yeah that's great that you are taking a half day. Half days are good. You know we all need them sometimes."

"Holly?" Okay, now he was really concerned.

"I love when I work half days. It's like a nice reprieve from Mildred. So it's almost like a vacation." She started to bounce on her feet.

"Holly, you're rambling."

"I am?" Her eyes widened. "I didn't realize. Are you sure? Maybe it's you that's rambling. I'm fine. I'm calm as a cucumber that's not about to be cut up and thrown into a salad for someone to eat."

That's it, he was calling the doctor. He gave her the once-over, assessing she was physically okay. Mentally on the other hand...

He shook his head as he walked over to the bag that was flung across the room.

"Stop!"

At Holly's scream, Ben froze. He slowly turned back to face her. That's when he saw the terror in her eyes. "Holly?"

"Don't look in there!"

"In where..." Ben reached for the bag. "Here?" Ignoring her protest, he looked at whatever was making his somewhat sane wife hysterical.

That's when his heart stopped.

*O*H *G*OD, *oh God, oh God. What do I do?*

Ben wasn't supposed to be home yet. The dogs were barking like they were being murdered. Her heartburn was back in full force, she was positive she was about to vomit. Her knees hurt. And now Ben looked like he'd short-circuited.

Seriously, right now Ben looked like he'd left his body and was replaced with a robot.

Holly's whole body started to go into hyperdrive. *Universe, can you not give me a freakin' break? Ever?*

Ben pulled the box from the bag. "Holly, what is this?"

"It's not what it looks like!" she screamed.

He arched his brow at her. "Really, because this looks exactly like a pregnancy test to me. Or is this how they're packaging candy nowadays?"

Holly looked at him in absolute horror, then she did what she did best. Holly word vomited. And she word vomited hard. "Okay yeah, so here's the thing, over the past two months I've been feeling weird, and kinda off and stuff and I couldn't write and whatever, no matter how hard I tried. I just couldn't do it. One day I was talking to Mildred and she was all," Holly mimicked Mildred, "you're unsettled and shit like that and I was all, no you're a crazy old woman." Holly started to pace. "Then Mildred left this book on my desk that had a baby on it and I was like holy shit I want a baby. I mean doesn't it sound perfect? Can you imagine a little blue-eyed baby running around here that looked exactly like you? I can." She stopped moving.

"Oh, but man, I really hope they don't get my klutz gene." Deciding not to look at him she continued with her pacing. "I was going to bring it up after we left my dad's that night, but then the break-in happened and I just never got to it. Fast forward to today and Mildred is all blah blah blah, you are already baking a bun, and at first, I didn't realize what that meant but then I got it and thought back to when I had my last period and I freaked. I left work and ran to the store and fell through the front door just now." She was entirely out of breath by the time she finished.

She stopped pacing long enough to brave a chance and look at Ben.

Yep. She broke him.

"Ben?" He stared back at her with an unreadable expression. "Uhh, Ben, you're starting to freak me out here."

"You're pregnant?" He finally mustered up some words.

As they stared at each other something shifted in the room. Quietly she answered him. "I don't know. Maybe."

Before Holly could register it, Ben was throwing her over his shoulder in a fireman's pose. "Hey, what the hell?"

"Bathroom," he stated.

Ben then ran them both to the bathroom before depositing Holly on the toilet. He then ripped open the box and shoved the stick at her. "Pee."

"Do not demand for me to pee." She glared at him. "I'm not a dog. I don't go on demand. Neither does Waffles, but you get what I'm saying."

"Holly, this is the moment we might find out if we are having a baby. Now pee."

"Not while you're in here!"

"I've seen all you got. Now, pee. Don't make me tell you again."

"Benjamin Richman, you leave this bathroom right now! If I'm gonna pee on a stick and it's gonna tell me if our lives are gonna be changed forever, then I am not doing that with you in here."

Ben glared at her. "The door stays open." He sidestepped out of the bathroom.

"*The door stays open,*" she mocked glaring at the spot Ben vacated.

She took a deep breath. *Oh my God.* Was she really about to do this?

Was Ben's reaction a good or bad thing? Did he want to know if she was pregnant so he could figure out what he needed to do with his life? What if he didn't want children right now?

What if she *was* pregnant?

Oh God, I might be pregnant.

I might be having a baby.

A real-life baby.

"I don't hear you peeing," Ben yelled from the other side of the wall.

"I can't pee under pressure!"

"Fine, I'm going to the kitchen."

Holly heard him stomp his feet. "I wasn't born yesterday. All you did was march in place."

"Holly just pee on the damn stick already so we can celebrate."

Celebrate?

At that exact moment, all of Holly's worries disappeared. Ben wanted to celebrate. He wanted a baby.

Holly took the stick in her hand and gave it a quick squeeze. *Here goes nothing.*

However, *nothing* ever went smoothly for her. She should have known better. As she hovered over the toilet, something nudged her leg.

Then it nudged harder.

When she focused, she saw Waffles at her feet. He then huffed before he jumped up on her leg. Unfortunately, for her, Holly was already unbalanced, but with Waffles sneak attack and her hand already being occupied she saw or rather felt it coming.

Timmmbbeeerrrr, she shouted in her head as she found herself falling through the air. In an attempt to catch herself, she grabbed onto the shower curtain, which effectively fell on top of her. Before she knew it, she was in the bathtub tangled in the curtain with her pants around her ankles.

Ben was instantly in the room. "Holy fuck, are you okay?" he asked, jumping into the shower to help her.

"Why does this stuff always happen to me?" She looked at him before darting her eyes to Waffles who had his two front paws on the side of the tub staring at her with his tongue hanging out of the side of his mouth.

"It's because you're Holly." Ben barked out a laugh.

"That's not a good enough reason."

He kissed her forehead. "It's all the reason you need. Are you hurt?"

"My ego, yes."

He raised his brows at her. "And?"

"And what?"

His gaze darted to the stick still in her hand. "Oh yeah." She was too afraid to really look at it. "I think I got enough on it but the box said we had to wait."

"Fine. Now, we wait." Ben pulled Holly out of the tub before unwrapping her from the shower curtain. "Finish up in here and then we'll read it together."

"Okay." Her mind was going a million miles an hour. And yet, she was still surprised her pants were down around her ankles.

Ben left the bathroom while Holly cleaned herself up.

Only me.

When she made it out of the bathroom, Ben had Ripley, Waffles, and Twitch all at his feet.

"What's with the party?" she asked, as she worried her bottom lip. It was like an intervention.

"If we are about to grow by one, I thought it was only fitting if everyone in the family was present."

"We don't know if I'm pregnant," she stated.

"True." He stared at her. "But if you are, everyone is here."

Holly nodded as her heart pounded. She took a deep breath before she held out her hand with the stick face up for both of them to read.

Chapter Ten

"WE'RE PREGNANT."

Ben stood there in awe as he watched an array of emotions run across Holly's face as she stared at the stick.

The stick that just changed their lives.

He must have been living in a dream world. It was as if everything stopped around them and all that was there was him and Holly.

The soon to be mother of his child.

His child.

Knocking him from his thoughts, Ben heard a whine come from his left. When he looked at his feet, he saw Ripley putting her paw in the air with her head tilted to the side trying to understand what was going on. He bent at his knee coming to eye level with all their pets who soon jumped into his arms nearly tackling him backward. "You guys ready to be big brothers and sisters?" he asked, making sure to scratch every one of them.

This was it. This was the moment he'd been waiting for his whole life.

With a yip from Waffles and Ripley, and a nudge on his

knee from Twitch, Ben's face broke into a ridiculously wide smile.

He was going to be a dad.

And not just to animals.

Ben looked up at his wife. She glowed, and the warm smile she sent back at him made his heart slam against his chest.

They were going to be parents.

This was the start of a new chapter for them.

Ben stood before he took a step closer to Holly cradling her face in his hands. He brought his lips to hers. He licked along her bottom lip demanding for her to open as he deepened their kiss.

Words wouldn't work at this moment.

Not when he was getting everything he ever wanted.

A baby.

They were going to have a baby.

He pulled back from their kiss to rest his forehead against Holly's. "We're going to be parents, Grace."

"We are." She smiled at him as tears formed in her eyes. When he saw a tear fall down her cheek, he used the pad of his thumb to gently wipe it away. "I love you, Holly Richman."

"I love you too, Ben." She stepped into his arms allowing him to enclose her in his embrace completely. Ben reached down grabbing her bottom forcing her to jump. Holly instinctually wrapped her legs around him.

The moment she was secured, he started making his way to their bedroom. Once he made it inside he kicked the door shut.

Sorry guys, but I'm on a mission and being interrupted is not in the plan.

Not this time.

Ben gently placed Holly on her back before moving down to her stomach. He then lifted her shirt before getting on his knees straddling her legs. Every so gently he placed the palm of his hand on her exposed skin.

My child is growing in here.

Ben was at a loss for words. He vowed at that moment he would do whatever it took to be the best father he could be. Just like his dad was to him, or how Henry was to Holly.

He would stop at nothing to make them proud.

Ben bent kissing Holly's stomach. *I will always protect you.*

"Uh, Ben?" Holly looked down at him. "You're kinda freaking me out here."

"Hush your face, can't you see I'm imagining you rounded with my child? Or children?" He winked at her.

"Take a step back there, mister. Child. Let's go with child as in singular."

"I want a whole sports team full," he said.

"Not out of my hoo-ha."

Ben laughed before kissing her stomach again. "We'll discuss it later. Have I told you today that I love you?"

"You tell me every day, but it's always nice to hear," she answered, looking at him with such love, he could feel it surrounding him.

His face brightened as he looked back at her. "I want to have many babies with you, Holly."

Holly's face softened with contentment as a twinkle in her eye appeared. "Good. 'Cause, Ben, I want to have many babies with you too."

A wicked smirk appeared on his face. "How do you think Waffles will handle it?"

Holly's eyes widened in shock. "I have no idea. Let's just hope for the best. The last thing we need is for him is to recruit our child as his minion in world domination."

"He'll probably try." Ben crawled up the bed to reach Holly. He then pulled her into another deep kiss. "I love you, baby." He moved from her lips as he peppered kisses along her jawline. "You've made me the happiest I've ever been."

"Ditto." A wicked grin appeared on her face. "Less talking, more celebrating."

"Oh, we are. Make no mistake of that." He growled.

Ben started to kiss along her exposed neck causing her to tilt her head back. Once he reached the collar of her shirt he sat up. "Off," he ordered as he pulled her shirt over her head forcing her to sit up.

"You're very demanding."

"Again, hush your face."

You know what? This is taking too long. He reached for the cups of her bra and ripped them in two. Holly then pushed at his chest. "Can you not destroy my clothes, please? I'm getting real tired of that."

He shrugged nonchalantly. "You took too long."

"You didn't even give me a chance!"

"Still took too long." He leaned over kissing her swollen chest. "How did I not notice these had grown?"

"I don't know. I mean I just thought I ate too many donuts." Holly's eyes rolled back into her head. "Donuts. Man, I would kill for a peanut butter glazed donut right now."

"Focus woman." Ben growled at her.

"But donuts."

He sat back on his heels. "You know it all makes sense now. You almost killed Waffles when he took one." He reached his hand out before pinching her nipple causing a slight moan to escape from her.

"I change my mind," she remarked. "No donuts, I want more suckie." She pushed her chest into the air.

"What momma wants, momma gets." Ben huffed out a laugh before he brought her peak into his mouth.

Man, he was so fucking lucky.

After a few seconds, he released her with a pop before moving to her other breast. He could do this for days. He let his tongue slide against her nipple before pulling away and blowing on it.

"Ben, please," Holly moaned.

"Patience," he said after releasing her. He then slid down her body before reaching her pants. In one quick movement, he pulled them, along with her panties from her body, throwing them behind him.

"At least you didn't rip them this time."

He cocked his brow at her. "Did you want me to?"

"Hell no!" Holly laughed as she let her legs fall open exposing her core to Ben.

Fuck, she was so beautiful.

Lightly he traced her lower lips with his fingertips feeling her wetness.

"Mhhmm." Holly threw her head back the moment Ben reached her clit. Bending over he brought it into his mouth causing Holly to shoot her hips to his face. Instantly she buried her hands in his hair as she rocked against his mouth.

"Ben," she cried.

He bit down on her clit before sucking it into his mouth

"Ben!" she screamed out. "Fuck me!"

"I plan on it." He used his fingers and pushed inside of her slowly. As her hips started to thrash around he knew she was close.

With one last lick of her core, he pulled back.

"Do you have a death wish?"

"Not today." He yanked his shirt over his head before undoing his belt buckle. He jumped from the bed discarding his pants.

Within seconds he was on top of her. "Is this what you want?" he growled as he positioned himself. Once he lined himself at her core, he slowly circled her entrance.

Holly narrowed her eyes at him. "Duh."

"Oh, you're feisty today, aren't you? You know I love it when you're feisty."

"No," she answered. "I'm horny and I believe since I'm now carrying your child and it wants me to eat nothing but peanut butter donuts, you better fuck me into burning off those calories."

He stopped what he was doing and arched his brow. "What?"

"For the love of all things. Cut me some slack." She bounced her head back and forth. "I can't think straight, right now."

"I'll let it slide this time," he said before inching his way inside of her. Honestly, he didn't have any other choice *but* to let it go. Seeing Holly so wanton, fucking unmanned him. And the fact inside of her was their child sent him over the edge.

Ben started slowly pushing his way inside of her as she clung to him. He gently grabbed her hips before flipping them so she'd be on top. After getting her situated he growled, "Ride me."

Without even a question Holly started moving her hips. Fuck he loved that she'd grown so comfortable with him to do so. He remembered when she used to try and hide herself from him.

Holly leaned back bracing her hands on his lower legs as she worked him up and down. Ben had to clench his teeth to keep control. With her legs spread wide, it gave him the perfect vantage point of their joining.

He couldn't stop himself even if he wanted to. He reached his left hand out opening her lower lips to expose her clit to his view. That's when Holly started to work herself harder as she moved around him.

"Oh God," she screamed. Ben started to feel her shake. He

was right there with her though. He could feel himself at his breaking point.

With one hand he pinched her clit while the other went to her hip helping with her movements.

He pounded himself into her as he felt Holly start to explode. Abandoning her clit, he lost all control as he slammed himself deep into her walls before bringing her hips down to his, and freezing. He groaned loudly as he emptied himself within her.

"Holy guacamole," Holly blurted out as she laid on top of him.

His sentiments exactly.

He did his best to calm his panting as he came down from his high. After a few minutes, Holly righted herself before looking down at him with a smile on her face that he was sure matched his own. He then let his gaze travel down to her stomach. He placed the palm of his hand on top of it. "I love you, Holly."

"I love you too, Ben."

Just then Ben's eyes widened. "Oh shit."

"What, what is it?" Holly asked as Ben rolled forcing her to fall off of him and onto her side.

Ben jumped from the bed and ran to his pants, grabbing his phone from the pocket. "Shit. There is so much to do."

"What's going on?" Holly pushed herself onto her elbows. "Are you okay? You're kinda freakin' me out here."

He snapped his attention to her at her worried voice. "Me. Yeah, I'm fine. It just hit me. Do you know how much shit you trip on and fall over every day? We're gonna have to Holly proof this house and pronto."

Ben looked back at his phone and started frantically typing. *There has got to be a place I can get a lot of it,* he thought.

"What are you doing?" Holly's brows were knitted together when Ben looked up.

"I'm searching the internet for bubble wrap. There's got to be a place where I can buy it in bulk." He gave her a 'duh' look. This was the most logical solution. Didn't she understand with her track record he was going to have to start *now* in Holly proofing the house?

"You are not covering this place in bubble wrap."

"Who said I was going to cover the place? That would be a waste of time." He looked her up and down cocking his brow.

"Oh no. No, you don't Benjamin. You are *not* wrapping me in bubble wrap. No freakin' way!"

"How else do you suppose I keep you safe?"

Holly jumped from the bed. As she made her way toward him, she banged her shin on the bedpost. "Owwie."

"See." He threw his phone on the bed before moving over to her and dropping to his knees. "Let me see."

"No." She refused to move her hand from her shin.

"Let me see, Holly."

"No. It's your fault I hit the dang thing anyway. We find out we're pregnant and then you go all crazy. So, no. I'm not moving my hand." She glared at him.

Ben rolled his eyes before he pushed her hand away himself. Thankfully there was only a small red mark. "It doesn't look like you cut it."

"Of course, I didn't cut it," she growled. "Let's get back to where you think it's a good idea for me to be wrapped up like some sort of lunch meat then—"

"You don't wrap lunch meat in bubble wrap."

"Can I use bubble wrap to clean up the mess I make once I strangle you to death?" Her lips thinned as she threw her hands on her hips angrily.

Ben sat back on his feet as he observed her. Damn, she was

fucking beautiful. Her hair was all over the place, her face red with annoyance.

And, she was going to be the mother of his children.

He was never going to forget this moment.

Ben pulled her body to his as he rested his head on her stomach. After a few seconds, Holly's hand moved to his hair. Once he realized she wasn't trying to rip out his hair, he smiled. Plus, she didn't need to know he already ordered the bubble wrap.

Ben picked her up at her waist and tossed her back onto the bed.

Round two.

"No manhandling." She glared at him. "How many times do I have to tell you?"

"I'm gonna manhandle you all right." However, as he reached for her hips his phone started to ring. "Shit."

"Answer it," Holly said. "It might be the insurance company."

Fuck. The last thing he wanted to do right now was to be pulled away from his wife. Especially when he registered Holly had lifted one of her breasts before toying with her nipple.

Fuck me.

Ben growled as he answered the phone. "Richman."

"Ben, it's Will."

Chapter Eleven

RIGHT AS HOLLY and Ben started their walk up the police station steps, they saw John burst through the door.

What the... Why the hell is he here? Holly's face scrunched at the sight. *Please don't tell me he was up to no good.* Holly gave him the once-over. Who was she kidding, this was John. Of course, he was up to no good.

The moment John recognized her and Ben his whole face lit up in a boyish grin. Instantly, he ran down the steps in their direction. Once John was right in front of them, she noticed Ben's brows shoot to the sky as he looked at his best friend. "What are you doing here?"

"I can ask the same thing about you two?" John crossed his arms over his chest surprising Holly.

Defensive much?

Holly watched amazed as Ben and John did this weird speaking thing but without actually speaking.

Okay, Twilight Zone, here I am.

Ben broke the silence first. "Will asked if we could come down to the station. I guess he has some information." Ben shrugged. "He didn't go into detail over the phone."

"Hopefully, he's got good news." John lifted his chin.

That's when Holly started to notice something was off. As she took a closer look at John she realized he was fidgeting.

Hold up. Holly looked John up and down. He was nervous, there was no disputing that, but more importantly, he looked... normal. Hell, he even looked like he brushed his hair. And was that... Holy crap that was cologne. "John," she started a little taken aback. "You look like a normal human being, your hair is brushed, your clothes look good... I'm in shock." Holly's mouth curved into a smile. "I'm gonna go out on a limb here and say you weren't at the station trying to... how did you put it before? Oh, yeah, make it look like you had an exciting story or something insane like that." Holly's smile widened from ear to ear as she teased him.

"Hey," he protested. "It worked last time." John lifted his chin as he glared at her.

"Oh, Ben, I think little Johnny here is defensive."

"Settle down children." Ben gave them both a look. "John, if you're not here for some insane logic that only *you* have, then why are you here? I'm pretty positive people don't hang out at the police station just for shits and giggles."

John sighed loudly as he looked behind him at the front door. When he looked back at her and Ben he shook his head. There was this overwhelming sense of disappointment coming from him. "I had to take care of something."

"Do I need to worry?" Ben asked, looking him up and down.

In an instant, John's demeanor changed and his signature boyish grin appeared back on his face. He then took off past them only looking back to shout, "Not yet. See ya later." He waved.

What the hell?

Everything happened so fast, it almost gave Holly

whiplash. They stood there in shock as John disappeared from sight. "Ben, what just happened?"

"I have absolutely no idea," he answered. "I have a feeling we'll find out soon."

"Why is he strange?" Holly scrutinized her husband. "Better yet, why do *you* attract the strange ones? There's me, you know, crazy dog, walking disaster, cannot tie my own shoes without falling over... And then there's John? I don't even have words to describe him. You must have this homing beacon for the weird ones."

Ben's eyes twinkled with amusement as he smirked at her. "I wish I had an answer for you, Grace. I stopped trying to make sense of it and decided I'd just roll with the punches. It's safer that way."

"Safer for who?"

"My sanity." A ridiculously wide smile appeared on his face.

"Ehh, you're probably right," she agreed. "It's probably better that way." Holly looked back at the police station and her gut twisted. She took a deep breath trying to shake the feeling that something terrible was going to happen. Or, you know, that might have just been her heartburn coming back.

Right now, it was a crapshoot.

At least she now knew what was causing her constant indigestion.

Whoa. The thought hit her. *I'm pregnant. Holy freakin' crap on a cracker.*

Ben squeezed her hand drawing her attention to him. "You okay, babe?" he asked, his brows knitted together in concern.

Even though inside she felt like she was a jumbled mess, knowing that Ben would be there through everything made her feel better. No matter what happened, they had each other.

She smiled warmly at him as she squeezed his hand. "Yeah, I think I'm just a little nervous. No one wants to come to a police station. Unless you're John or something." Then a new thought hit her sending a wave of ice down her back. "Oh, shit sticks." Holly took a step back as her face paled. "What if Officer Jones is in there?"

Ben's hand went to his stomach as he barked out a deep laugh. "What am I going to do with you?" He shook his head as he took a step pushing her toward the front door. I'm sure you'll be fine. Just don't speak to him and I think you'll avoid him throwing you in handcuffs again."

Holly pointed at her mouth as her eyes narrowed. "I can't stop what comes out of here. You know that."

"Try." Ben leaned forward and kissed the top of her head. "You're gonna have to start to learn to curb your word vomits anyway or our little peanut will pick them up."

Peanut. She liked that. She placed the palm of her hand on her stomach. "Let's hope Peanut doesn't get any of my traits."

Before Holly could register what was going on, Ben pulled her to face him. He brought his lips down to her in a possessive kiss taking her breath away. "Don't say that," he growled. "I want Peanut to have all the best parts of you."

She loved this man more than anything. A half-smile appeared on Holly's face. "Just not the falling over part, right?"

"We might not be able to avoid it." Ben playfully winked at her. "According to Henry, your mother was just like you."

"True. If peanut gets my stumbling gene, you're gonna have to ask my dad for some tips on how he dealt with two walking catastrophes." Her eyes went round, as the thought hit her. "We need to tell my dad!" Holly started fumbling through her bag looking for her phone.

Ben grabbed her hand bringing it to his lips. "Let's work

on one thing at a time. What if Will's gonna inform us everything is done and we can go on with our lives?"

"That would be nice."

"It would, now let's go find out." Ben started walking up the stairs holding Holly's hand.

The moment Ben opened the door, Holly saw one of the clinic's regular clients. "You're Bruce's mom!" Holly exclaimed, pulling out of Ben's grasp. "It's good to see you again." Holly turned back to Ben. "Why didn't you tell me she worked here?"

"Please, Mrs. Richman call me Emma." Emma gave Holly a welcoming smile, which Holly returned.

"And you call me Holly." She smiled brightly at her, however after a few seconds, Holly noticed Emma kept looking behind them.

To make sure she wasn't missing anything Holly did the same. When she didn't see anyone she turned back to Emma who was now looking at Ben.

"Is he with you again?" Emma asked as she looked behind them one more time.

"Is who with us?" Holly once again turned and saw no one.

Emma sent Ben a strained look as she worried her bottom lip.

"Wait, do you mean John?" Ben quirked a single brow at her.

Emma's pale face colored as her gaze dropped. "Uh, yeah." She then started fidgeting with her fingers. "I mean he just left, but when I saw you two come in I figured he might have snuck back in."

Holly's mouth fell open. "John was kicked out of here?"

Emma looked back at her desk as she shyly placed a piece of her honey brown hair behind her ear. "Well, technically no. He wasn't kicked out per se. I mean I'm sure if I did call one of the officers I could have gotten them to fill out the paperwork, but he doesn't need to know I didn't really call them. I only fake called them."

"Is John bothering you?" Ben asked.

"Not really, well kinda." Emma snapped her attention to the computer screen in front of her. "Umm, hey, you know what? No need for us to talk about that. What can I do for both of you? I'm sure you two are here for something other than to talk about me."

Uhh, say what? Holly looked around the room to see if she was missing something.

"Detective Bower called us not long ago and asked us to come see him," Ben remarked, distracting Holly from her search.

So, we are ignoring this? She looked at him.

"Oh, good good, that's a good thing." Emma looked back at Ben. "He must have more information on the case." Then Emma started to ramble. "I still can't believe someone would ever do that to Richman Veterinarian Hospital. I mean seriously you are the best vet in town, why would anyone want to do anything to you? And the poor animals. I'm just glad all of them turned out okay. If someone had done anything to even one of them, there would have been hell to pay." Her face hardened as her nostrils flared. "Can you believe the audacity of some people? A poor defenseless animal has no chance when it comes to stupid assholes. I mean sometimes humans can't defend themselves either but we can try. I guess animals can try too, but sometimes bad things happen to good people and it takes a long time, if ever, to get put back together again." She took a deep breath. "And then, what if, when you're trying to be put back together you end up with a dog that's got all the same issues as you? I guess it's funny how the Universe works that way, right? You get a big dog to help make you feel safe, but it turns out he's just like you so you both end up jumping at all the same things." Emma's eyes widened in shock.

"Emma?" Ben's face softened.

Holly darted her eyes to Ben trying to make any sense of the situation. *What is going on?* Holly looked back at Emma who now looked like she'd seen a ghost. At seeing the shame buried in her eyes, Holly's heart twisted. Call it her newly found motherly instincts or whatnot, but all Holly wanted to do was pull Emma into her arms and tell her everything was going to be okay.

Ben glanced at Holly, his eyes telling her to leave it be and they'll talk about it later.

She looked back at Emma and her heart broke.

"Detective Bower." Emma interrupted Holly's thought. "Yes, you are here to see him. Let me send him a quick message and let him know you're on your way back." She looked at Ben with the mask slipped over her face. "Do you remember where it is?"

Ben nodded. "I believe so, it's down the hall, right?"

"Yep." Emma turned back to her computer. However, Holly noticed Emma sunk deeper into her chair as if to make herself appear smaller.

Holly couldn't take it anymore.

Ben must have known what she needed because he gave her a subtle nod and walked toward the back leaving her at the reception desk. "You okay, Emma?"

"Of course, I'm fine." Emma forced a fake smile on her lips. "Sorry about that, it's been a little bit of a difficult morning."

"Is John bothering you, Emma?" Holly tried her best to sound comforting without pity. "He's a pain in the ass but he's a good guy." Deciding to lighten the mood Holly winked at her. "If he's done anything to upset you, I've got a friend that has connections. You say the word, and I'll make him go away."

Emma's face paled. "What? Oh, God no. John's fine. You don't have to do anything."

"Good." Holly let out a dramatic breath. "To tell you the truth, she scares me, and even though I'm not one hundred percent certain if she really does have connections or not. I really don't want to find out. Then there's the fact, John is Ben's best friend. He might be a pain in the ass but I don't think Ben wants to break in someone else."

Emma stared at her for a second before a smile spread across her face. "Oh, I get it, you're joking with me." Emma sat back in her chair. "You had me going there for a minute."

"Sure, we'll say it as a joke." Holly smiled. No need to scare the poor girl any further and tell her about Mildred. Yet.

"Besides, I think this was all a little misunderstanding," Emma remarked. "John is a nice guy, and he's not really bothering me per se. He's just uhh, I don't really have the right word for it."

"I think what you are looking for is, 'much'. John's a little much."

Emma threw her pointer finger in the air. "Yes, that's a perfect way to describe it. Let's go with much."

Holly watched Emma relax.

There was something about Emma that Holly really liked. She'd always thought that. Anytime her and Bruce had come into the clinic while Holly was there, she'd always gotten a good feeling about her, even if she was standoffish. "How's Bruce?"

Emma's whole face brightened at the mention of her dog. "He's good. He's Bruce, that's all I can really say about him. How's your Corgi?"

Holly shrugged. "Ehh, he's still plotting his world domination."

"He does have that kind of aura about him, doesn't he?"

"That's an understatement, Emma," Holly laughed. She liked Emma. A lot. Without thinking Holly reached over the side of the desk and grabbed a pen from a cup, she then grabbed the notepad that was lying on top. She scribbled her phone number down before handing it back to Emma. "Here, take this. Maybe we can do lunch or something?"

"Oh, well, I—"

Holly cut her off. "We can spend the time gossiping about how insane John is. I've got lots of stories."

A sad smile appeared on Emma's face. "That's very kind of you, but I don't need to know anything about John. I'm sure in a couple of weeks he'll forget all about me and trying to ask me on a date."

"That's why John was here!" Holly squealed, causing Emma to jump.

"No, no, I said that wrong. I mean to say he was—"

"No takie backie," Holly laughed. "Ben and I were trying to figure out why he was here. Now we *have* to have lunch."

"I don't think that's a good idea."

"Why not?" Holly arched her brow. "You've got the perfect inside scoop right here." She pointed at herself. "What's better than having the wife of his best friend at your disposal?"

Emma held up her hands. "Whoa, umm let's take a step back here."

"Plus," Holly continued ignoring Emma's worried expression. "I'm gonna need girl talk. Real honest to God girl talk. I spent most of my time taking care of my dad, so all I've got is this two-hundred-year-old woman that makes overly inappropriate comments all the time. Sure, I love her but I need someone my age to help me through all of this." She pointed at her belly.

"All of what, do you have a stomachache?" Emma's face scrunched.

"We just found out I'm pregnant." She placed her hand on her stomach before snapping her eyes back to Emma. "Whoa, now you have to have lunch with me. You're the first person I've told."

"I am?" Emma's brows shot up in shock before she recovered. "Congratulations!" She jumped from her seat causing the chair to hit the wall. Emma then ran around the desk pulling Holly into her arms. "A baby is amazing news. I've always wanted one."

Emma jumped back from their embrace. "I'm sorry that was inappropriate of me."

"No, it wasn't." Holly pulled her back into a hug.

That was it, Emma might not have known it yet, but she just sealed her fate in joining their *weird club*. She'd fit in perfectly, though, she had a dog that was *different* add that in with Holly's pets and it was like a friendship made in heaven.

"Congratulations again," Emma said, pulling out of Holly's arms.

"Thank you, it's still kinda unreal. We only just found out before Will called." A daze washed over Holly's face before remembering why they were there. "Oh crap. Ben's probably waiting for me."

"You're right." Emma stepped behind the front desk. "It's right down the hall on the left."

Holly smiled at her before she started walking toward the back. However, Emma stopped her, holding out a piece of paper. "Uhh, here's my number. I'd really like to have lunch one day."

Holly took it with a wide smile. "Consider it done." She placed the paper into her back pocket and with an extra pep in her step, she started walking down the hall. She could see her and Emma forming a friendship. Plus, it'd be fun to hear more about this whole John thing.

However, the moment Holly turned the corner she paled. There right in front of her was Officer Jones.

Oh shit.

Chapter Twelve

Ben sat in Will's office as they waited for Holly. This had been the second time Emma had rambled on about her past. Even though Ben could only speculate, he had a pretty good idea what was going on. Maybe Emma needed someone to talk to? And taking one look at his wife, he knew Holly was on the same page as him.

Ben's brows drew together as he thought about it. On second thought, maybe leaving her with Emma was a bad thing. Holly did tend to get a little overprotective at times.

Yeah, this was a bad idea.

The moment he was about to go look for her, Holly came charging into the room. Her face pale and her eyes were wide. So wide you'd have thought she'd seen a ghost.

"You okay, babe?" Ben jumped up from his seat. Maybe something was wrong with her or the baby. *Did she fall? Run into a wall?* They were two solid possibilities.

"Yeah, yeah." Holly brushed her shirt down avoiding eye contact with him. "I'm fine. Just ran into someone I was hoping to avoid," she answered as she pushed her hair out of her face giving him a forced smile. "But I'm here now."

Holly walked right past Ben refusing to look at him before taking a seat in front of Will's desk.

Ben cocked his brow. *Well, okay then, at least she didn't hurt herself. That I know of...*

"It's good to see you again, Holly," Will remarked, standing to shake her hand. "Ben was telling me you two have been quite worried about the break-in."

Holly's eyebrows shot to the ceiling in surprise. "Did he also tell you he wants to add on a room to the house and bring home his patients at night?"

"No, he left that out." Will's eyes studied Ben.

"I was only contemplating it. I didn't say it was a done deal." Ben snapped his attention to his wife. *I'll remember this.* When all she did was shrug, Ben's eyes narrowed. *Oh, feisty again today I see.*

"Nope, I don't think that's quite right," Holly stated, with that mischievous look she always got when she wanted to rile him. Why she was doing it, he had no idea. But he was going to use it to his advantage later. "Ben, you were drawing up blueprints."

"Hey." Ben shrugged. "Can you blame me?"

Ben moved to the seat next to her where Holly placed her hand in his. "Never. It's actually quite endearing you care so much about your patients. I'm just giving you a hard time. I'm nervous, so I'm rambling."

Ben leaned over and kissed her cheek. "This just means instead of one room I get to build two now."

One point for Ben.

Holly's lips thinned.

Zero for Holly.

Will sat back in his chair scrutinizing both of them. "Truthfully, I'm not all that surprised you're considering other alternatives. We've seen this before. Especially, when the break-in had no rhyme or reason. You feel like you need a new sense of security. It's very common."

"It doesn't make any sense. If someone broke in to steal something as fucked up as it sounds, I would at least feel more at ease," Ben replied, shrugging at Holly's swat to his arm at his language. It clearly didn't faze him since he continued, "You know, when someone gets their house broken into, it's usually for somebody to steal their stuff. This is a mystery even after weeks, we still can't find anything missing."

Will scratched his chin as his brows pulled together in thought. "I'll be honest here. It was extremely odd there was nothing tampered with or missing. That's why I've asked you both to come in today. We believe we now know the motive and have a suspect in mind." Will placed two still photos captured from the surveillance camera outside of the clinic in front of Holly and Ben. "Over the past few weeks we've been going over the information, and the footage my men retrieved."

Ben took one of the photos in his hand, but he couldn't make out the quality well enough to see anything.

"It was hard to recognize the suspect at first, but there was something familiar about him." Will turned his computer monitor toward Ben and Holly and hit play. That's when Ben saw a child maybe fifteen or sixteen take something and smash it through the clinic's front window.

"Oh God," Holly whispered from beside him.

The feed then showed the kid jump through the smashed window as he disappeared into the clinic. Then, seemingly out of nowhere, another child this one much younger than the first, maybe seven came into view. Instead of following the older one into the clinic he bounced around on his feet and worried his hands together.

As Ben watched the screen, he couldn't help the feeling there was something off about this younger child. He looked scared. But not in the way they might get caught scared, it was more than that.

Then the young child looked directly at the camera.

Ben's gut tightened. He was right, there was so much more in his eyes. There was an underlying of pain, mixed in with terror.

Before Ben could study him more, the footage morphed to the inside of the clinic. The older one that had smashed in the window was tearing the place apart. He was flipping tables over, throwing pamphlets around, you name it, he was doing it. He even spit on the floor of the waiting room.

Then, the boy jumped back through the window plowing into the younger kid making him fall on the ground. The first boy jumped up not caring to help the younger one, turned back to the clinic, gave it the finger and then took off running, leaving the younger boy on the ground holding his elbow in pain.

After thirty seconds, the younger one slowly got to his feet before looking all around.

Ben watched as the boy looked back at the camera with an almost pleading face before limping away in the opposite direction as the first kid.

"Holy crap." Holly grabbed Ben's hand and squeezed.

"At first, before we looked at the footage, we were under the assumption this might have been a neighborhood prank. Then once my guys went frame by frame, we pulled out this." Will took one of the papers on his desk and turned it over.

Ben and Holly both leaned forward to get a better look at what Will had uncovered.

"That's the kid that poisoned Twitch!" Holly jumped from her chair causing it to flip backward.

"You're right." Ben picked up the photo taking a better look at it. He never saw the kid in person, other than the news coverage. During the trial, they used his findings and toxicology reports to seal their investigation.

The only reason the case got media attention to begin with was because of Ben's mother leaving Richman Industries without any notice. Since the news put together Ben and the poisoned kitten, they did everything they could to get some inside scoop about what was really going on.

Ben had spent his whole life trying to avoid anything with Richman Industries, and leave it to the media outlets to do absolutely anything to connect stories, even where there was zero a connection.

"You're correct," Will agreed. "I've had to deal with him quite a few times in the past."

"You'd mentioned something like that when you dropped Twitch off." Ben sat back in his chair.

"So why did he do it?" Holly asked as she righted her seat.

With a heavy sigh, Will began, "Apparently, he blames you for all his troubles now."

"Me? All I did was confirm what he'd done to Twitch."

"Yes, but with the stuff that went down at Richman Industries, the news was all over 'the kid who poisoned the wealthiest man in the city's cat, just to see what would happen'. He holds you personally responsible for him being sentenced to the Juvenile Detention Center."

"I didn't ask for the news to follow the story. Hell, we weren't even aware of it until we saw it one night scrolling through the channels." Ben scrunched his face.

"Yeah, so now in his twisted brain he wants revenge on Ben and the clinic?" Holly asked.

"That appears to be the motive." Will sat back in his chair.

"Okay, so now what?" Ben still couldn't wrap his head around the fact this kid was the one that broke into the clinic and more importantly he did it to get back at him.

"That's the thing. We were able to locate the other boy in

the video, but not the one that poisoned Twitch. We don't know if this one incident was his payback or if he has more planned," Will answered. "Since nothing has happened since the break-in this might have been just a one time occurrence but I wanted you both to be aware of the situation at hand right now."

"Do you think he's dangerous?"

"I don't, but I do think he feels wronged. That combination, with his unfortunate track record, does raise some concerns." Will looked at them. "Do I think he will come after you to cause harm? No. Is there always that possibility? Yes. Unfortunately, that's the way it is with these situations."

"I don't get it. So, you brought us in here to tell us it was the kid who poisoned our cat, but we don't need to worry, but then we also do until you find him?" Holly rushed out. "Why can't you find him? You're a detective, that's your job. You *detect* things such as this child who now has a vendetta against my husband because of the news making him the center of attention." Holly snapped her gaze to Ben. "What if this kid decides he needs more revenge and comes after you or me. I mean he's just a child but he *poisoned* Twitch. He tried to kill him. Kill. Him. Ben! We can't go around worrying about what else he might do." Tears formed in Holly's eyes. "What if he does something to me or the baby?"

"You're pregnant?" Will interrupted Holly's tirade.

Ben wrapped his arms around Holly's shoulders bringing her to him. He then looked at Will. "Yes. We only found out a few hours ago."

"Congratulations."

"Thanks." Ben cradled Holly in his arms. "Holly does make a good point though. Are you still looking for him? What is it that we need to do?"

"We have a hunch of where he's been hiding out."

"Then why haven't you arrested him yet?" Holly glared at him as her nostrils flared.

Ben moved his attention to Holly. *I guess these are the pregnancy mood swings I've always heard about.*

"That's where we have a little problem."

"What problem?"

"Do you remember that other child in the footage?" Will handed Ben the other photo.

"Yeah."

"I have concerns about him. We were able to easily locate him in our system. He was placed in the city's foster care system two years ago when both of his parents were killed in a motor vehicle accident. He apparently had no other living relatives."

No wonder he looked downright terrified.

He suddenly had the urge to vomit. Ben was much older when he lost his father, but that had gutted him. He couldn't imagine how he would feel if at such a young age it would have been to lose his father.

"He lost both of his parents?" Holly placed her hand on Ben's knee squeezing it.

"Yes." Will's expression changed to sorrow. "He's been bounced from foster home to foster home every few months."

"Why are you telling us this?" Ben asked as he heard a sniffle come from Holly.

"Yeah, and why are you concerned about him?" Holly asked, wiping away the tear from her eyes. "Sorry, I normally don't cry this easily."

"Martha cried at everything when she was pregnant, then in a split second she'd be throwing something at my head."

"That sounds like something fun to look forward to," Ben mumbled.

"I got pretty good at dodging," Will chuckled before going

serious. "Jimmy, the young boy in foster care might be in jeopardy of the other boy lashing out at him."

"Why?"

"Unfortunately, the suspect needs someone to blame in his life and I fear he might turn his anger onto Jimmy."

"Then get the city to move him somewhere else?"

"It doesn't quite work that way, Mrs. Richman." Will sat straighter in his chair.

"Well, that's dumb." Holly crossed her arms over her chest.

"I agree, but my hands are tied. I reached out to his social worker to see what we can do. But in the meantime, we're monitoring this situation closely. As soon as we can safely move forward, I wanted to at least give you both the heads up."

Ben stood reaching his hand out to Will. "I appreciate you taking the time to inform us."

"Yes, thank you." Holly stood. She worried her bottom lip. "Jimmy, you said his name was, right?"

"Yes."

"He looked like he got hurt. Was he okay?"

"Other than a few scrapes and cuts, he seemed fine."

Holly nodded but Ben could see she still had questions. "Why was he with the other boy to begin with?"

Ben had that same question.

Will sighed. "According to the recent reports from Jimmy's social worker, he's lost. After losing his parents, he's done anything he can to feel like he belongs somewhere. Which isn't uncommon for children in the system. He sadly just met the wrong kid."

Ben let the words register as he felt Holly's whole body slump. "Thank you," she said.

"Try not to worry. We will get it all worked out." Will gave Holly a sweet smile. "And congratulations again on the baby.

Having a child was the most rewarding thing I've ever done in my life. I wouldn't change it for the world. Even with all the complications that arose."

"Thank you," Ben replied. "Keep us posted, okay?"

"You'll be the first I contact."

Chapter Thirteen

BEN SAT in his office trying to fill out his reports for the day but was ending up nowhere. No matter how hard he tried he couldn't focus.

He sat back in his chair with a groan as he closed his eyes. Especially after a day like today. As soon as he arrived in the office, he was greeted with a hit and run.

Those were the cases that always twisted him. But at the same time, knowing him and his team were the ones that could help save an animal is what he thrived on.

Plus, when you add in the fact a human could hit an animal and then just drive off with no remorse had him seeing red. Call him out of the ordinary, but he didn't get it. Maybe it was his love of animals or whatever? But it pissed him off. Hell, if it were up to Ben, the people that did commit hit and runs on animals *or* humans they deserved the highest form of punishment.

He opened his eyes. *You know, I could lobby for that.*

Then again... he scratched the scruff on his chin. That would take away from what he loved to do, and being there to help save the animals that were hurt was more important.

He looked back at his screen seeing the files on the Basset Hound that had been hit.

He couldn't deny he loved the rush that came from cases like this, though. That quick action, think on your feet and do everything you could to save a life, was the kind of high he liked.

And lucky for him, he had the best team at his side when things got intense.

Sadly, they'd gotten a lot of practice over the years when it came to animals getting hit by cars. Just in the last six months, they'd had about five cases. People had gotten so careless while driving, completely engrossed in their phones, posting social media updates, texting, taking photos, you name it. And when you focused more on the tiny device in your hand rather than the two-ton vehicle you were in control of, it was a recipe for disaster.

In many ways.

Thankfully, as Ben skimmed through his document, he was able to smile at the outcome. The Bassett Hound had survived, with only a few injuries and was right now, in one of the cages in the back recovering.

Today was a good day, though.

Sometimes these cases didn't have happy endings.

Having to tell the owners their family member didn't make it never got easier.

Thankfully today that wasn't the case. Instead, Ben was able to walk out into the waiting room, where the dog's owners, a man and woman in their mid-thirties along with their young son refused to go home and tell them 'Bob the Dog,' was going to make it.

Days like today were the days he knew he made a difference.

He sat back in his chair with a smile on his face. Plus, today was going to end with a bang.

Tonight, Holly and Ben had decided on telling Henry about the baby.

At first, Ben wanted to wait until after their doctor's appointment, but Holly didn't. Maybe it was the medical professional in him or whatever, but he wanted solid proof that everything was okay and as it should be.

Sure, peeing on a stick was helpful, but it didn't give all the answers he wanted or needed.

As he relaxed in his chair he couldn't help but laugh. Their compromise was one for the books if you asked him.

"You have got to be kidding me, Benjamin Richman." Holly glared at him as he ushered her into the lobby of the clinic.

"Do you think I'd joke about something like this?"

"That's what worries me," she admitted. "First there is this. Then who knows what else your brain is gonna come up with."

Ben did have to admit he was overreacting a tad, but after everything that went down at the police station, he had this unsettled and worried feeling running through him. No matter what he did, he couldn't escape it. Maybe, it was all the adrenaline of the situation and the information revealed, but he hoped in doing this he'd get some sort of relief. "Shirt up, pants down, and up you go."

"Déjà vu," Holly remarked, narrowing her eyes at him.

"I don't recall me telling you to undress when you busted your lip and chipped your tooth."

"You mean when you busted my lip."

"The frisbee did, not me."

"You were the one that threw it."

"And you were the one that didn't get out of the way when I yelled watch out." He cocked his left brow at her. "Grace, we can do this all night if you want."

"If only you said those words to me the first time."

"I was thinking it, trust me," he growled, looking at his wife.

Holly threw her top over her head tossing it to the seat in the room leaving her in her bra. She then pushed down her pants exposing her lower abdomen.

"Good." Holly looked at him with lust in her eyes. "Me too."

"Don't play with fire, Grace."

"Or what, I'll get burned?"

"Don't you know it." Ben helped her onto the exam table before leaving the room to retrieve the portable ultrasound device he had in the clinic. Once he made it back he saw Holly sitting on the edge of the table with her hand on her stomach.

It was a surreal feeling.

And to think this was all where it started.

She looked at him with the right side of her mouth curved upward. "Once you do whatever the hell it is you need to do, you think we can tell my dad? He'll be super excited. I think he's been waiting for this moment since I hit puberty."

Ben huffed out a laugh as a smile spread across his face. "I'm not the least bit surprised." He walked over to her motioning for her to lean backward. When she did he placed the gel on to her stomach.

"Fuck me, that's cold. Could you have warmed it up?"

"Oops."

"Don't oops me, mister. Drop your pants and let me squirt that shit on your balls. I bet you'll never forget to warm it up again."

As he opened his mouth she stopped him. "And don't tell me you only use this on animals. They feel the cold just like we do."

"Yes, dear." He had to bite his lip to keep from smiling.

Within a few seconds of searching with the wand, everything froze around him as his heart melted. There in front of him, was indeed a baby.

His *baby growing inside of his wife.*

He looked back at Holly tears forming in his eyes.

"What, what's wrong? Oh God, is something not okay? Does

it have horns? I mean if it did that's okay, I would still love it just the same. But I'm kinda freaking out here."

Only Holly.

Ben placed the portable device in front of her. "No, Grace, no horns or extra limbs."

The room fell silent as Holly focused on the screen in front of her. This was it, this was their baby. This was the start of their new li—

"I don't know what I'm looking at!" Holly cried, interrupting his thoughts.

"You're looking at our baby."

"No, I'm looking at black and white lines on a screen the size of a tiny computer." She looked at him, tears escaping from her eyes. "I'm such a bad mom already. Waffles walks all over me. Ripley only listens to you. Twitch thinks I'm only his food source, and now I can't see my own child. I'm the worst mom ever!"

Ben let go of the wand bringing Holly into his arms as he did his absolute best not to laugh, but was failing miserably.

"Are you laughing at me?" She cried harder.

"Baby...shh." He kissed the top of her head as he comforted her. "You are not a bad mom. Not to our pets and not to this one right here." He picked up the wand finding their baby again. "Do you see that round thing right there in the middle of the screen?"

"Yeah." She sniffled.

"That's our baby."

"Really?" Holly looked at it closer. "Well, I saw that!"

"See you did see our baby." Ben kissed her forehead.

"I did, didn't I." Holly straightened as she puffed out her chest. "I'm a good mom."

"Yes, baby. The best."

Ben laughed at the memory. Leave it to Holly to make everything a chaotic adventure.

Everything.

Between her and Waffles he never knew which end was up.

As he settled back into his paperwork for the night, that feeling of unease or whatever it was came back. Actually, it never went away. Instead over the last few days it had only gotten stronger.

Sure, seeing their baby had helped some, but it was something else. Something he couldn't put his fingers on.

Ben looked around his office once more. He couldn't stop himself from going back to the night of the break-in. And now knowing who had committed it, didn't sit well with him.

The *whole* thing didn't sit well with him. What if this kid wanted to cause him more problems? Now that Holly was pregnant, things changed.

Then his mind drifted to what Will had said about the other boy that was there.

The feeling he had came back in full force, like a punch to the gut.

Seeing that child stare into the camera with so much pain and sorrow in his eyes, did something to Ben.

Then there was the terror.

The little boy who had already gone through so much in his life.

Then seemingly out of nowhere a picture popped into his head making him choke.

Ben's head pounded as his palms started to sweat.

Holy shit. Holy fucking shit. Ben's breathing increased.

The picture in his mind was plain as day. It was of him and Holly carrying their baby in her arms, Waffles, Ripley and Twitch at their feet, but what really sent Ben sputtering all around was seeing that little boy by their side.

Jimmy.

Ben blinked a few times trying to get his brain to work, but every time he closed his eyes, he saw it again.

"That's it." Ben pushed out of his seat before closing down his computer. "No more coffee this late at night."

What the absolute hell was that? Ben could feel his heart still racing. And even though he felt like he'd just completed a triathlon, for the first time since leaving the police station that feeling he had slowly started to dissipate.

He took a deep breath trying to calm himself.

You need to leave this office. Right now.

Ben did his best to push all of his thoughts away. He glanced down at his watch. Maybe he was delirious, he needed to leave anyway. Besides tonight was going to be a celebration. That's what he needed to focus on, and since he was already late, he was sure Holly was crawling out of her skin holding in their news.

Yes, focus on telling Henry. That's what you're going to do.

Quickly he locked everything up and set the alarm. Once he made it out of the back door, he closed his eyes still trying to calm himself.

That's when he saw the image again in his mind.

Shaking his head, he jogged over to his SUV and quickly got on the road. Maybe putting some distance between him and the clinic would help.

Pulling around the corner he saw Holly's favorite donut shop. *That's what I'll do.* He decided to stop and pick up a half dozen donuts in hopes that focusing on getting Holly her most craved food, his brain would settle.

Unfortunately for him, he never once stopped thinking about Jimmy.

Chapter Fourteen

LASAGNA.

Holly held the store-bought lasagna in her hand as she walked up the steps to her father's house with Ripley and Waffles trotting along next to her.

Maybe after eating this, my brain will go back to normal?

All day Holly had been out of sorts. At first, she thought she was nervous about telling her father they were expecting, but it seemed to be more than that. She just couldn't put her finger on it.

Then, as she pictured their future conversation while eating dinner, she got the strongest craving for lasagna she'd ever had.

So here she was carrying the thing hoping that once she had some, her brain would stop being a jumbled mess.

A mess that consisted of her having a child, being a mother, the break-in, Emma, her normal worry about her father, and now... now it screamed lasagna.

"Pumpkin!" Henry opened the door. "Whatcha got for me?"

Without registering it, Holly pulled the box to her chest with a growl. "Mine."

"Well, it looks like someone woke up on the wrong side of the bed." Henry gave her a look.

"Sorry, Dad. It's been a crazy few days."

"Come on in and tell me all about it." Waffles and Ripley zoomed past Henry as they made their way into the house. "At least they aren't grumpy."

"I'm not grumpy," she protested. Holly walked past her father only stopping to give him a kiss on the cheek before heading straight to the kitchen. "Just hungry."

Sure, she might not be able to cook, but she could damn well preheat an oven and throw in a frozen lasagna.

Well, there was that one time... No. This she could do. And even if she couldn't, so help the person that stopped her from grabbing a fork and going to town on the lasagna, frozen or not.

Once the food was in the oven, Holly turned. Unfortunately, for her, she didn't see that Waffles and Ripley were playing tug of war across the kitchen. She took one step before tripping over them both. "Oh, for the love of all things!" Holly caught herself on the nearby table.

"I'd like to say that was a record, but you've tripped coming up the stairs before."

"Very funny, Dad."

"I thought so."

She rolled her eyes. "Ben had to work late on paperwork, but he should be here by the time the food is done." Holly moved past her father and into the living room.

The more room between her and the lasagna... the better.

Holly's excitement about telling her dad about the baby came back in full swing. She wished Ben was here. She was nearly crawling out of her skin with anticipation. It took everything inside of her not to blurt out she was now the host for a small human creature.

If it were up to her, she would have told her dad the second she got here, but no... something about a special moment and togetherness, and if she told her dad without Ben there... and blah blah blah, she stopped listening the moment Ben threatened to take away her donuts.

The gall of him.

Jerk.

But she got it. She didn't have to like it, but she got it. She placed her hand on her stomach as she watched her father slowly move into the room before carefully getting into his chair.

"Is he still worried about the clinic being broken into again?" Henry asked, making himself comfortable.

"Yes and no. He had some paperwork to finish, but the other day the detective overseeing the case called us into the station with information."

Henry's brows shot to the ceiling, the best his left side could. "And you're only telling me this now?"

Oh crap.

"I'm sorry, Dad," she pleaded with him. "It's been such a busy few days."

You know finding out I'm having a child. Then there's the who in the break-in. Not to mention that poor little boy that—

"So busy you couldn't pick up the phone and tell your old man?" he interrupted her thoughts.

"Do you remember the reason I got Twitch was 'cause some kid poisoned him?"

"Yeah."

"Well, I guess it turns out, that same kid was the one that broke into the clinic."

"You're kidding?" Henry sat back in his chair staring at her.

"I'm not. He blames Ben for everything that happened. With all the stuff happening at Richman Industries the news wanted more of a story. Remember that? You know anything that could connect to the wealthiest man in the city or some crap like that."

"So, you're saying this young man, who I assume has been released from the detention center now is seeking revenge?"

"It seems that way."

"Well, I'll be damned."

As her father sat back in his chair, Holly's brain zoned back to Will's office. The same way it had done anytime she thought of the break-in. She didn't know why, but the image of the young boy looking up at the camera was forever ingrained in her brain.

Hell, it even haunted her dreams at night. There was this feeling about it she couldn't seem to put her finger on.

Doing what she'd done over the last few days she pushed it aside as she watched Waffles and Ripley play.

"Holly?"

She turned to her father only to see a concerned look on his face. "Yeah, Dad?"

"Have you listened to one word I've said?"

He was speaking?

"I've been talking to you for twenty minutes."

"You have?"

"Yes, you were nodding your head and agreeing about my thoughts on the situation."

Holly looked around the room. Had she really zoned out that much? "I'm sorry, Dad. What did you say?"

"Ehh, it's too much to go over it again." Henry tossed the tennis ball Waffles had laid at his feet across the room. "How about you tell me what's got you all distracted?"

"I'm not distracted."

Henry gave her the look. "Okay fine, I'm distracted."

"How about you throw your old man a bone here."

Waffles must have thought he meant he had bones because he ran to Henry jumping and barking.

"You sure are driven by food," Henry laughed, scratching Waffles behind the ears.

"He's just like his momma," Holly said looking back into the kitchen. Thank God she'd gotten a smaller lasagna and it should be done any moment now.

"I'm gonna tell Ben you said tha—"

"Sorry I'm late," Ben announced walking into the living room. "It's been one of those days."

Henry's face brightened seeing Ben. He then as carefully as he could stood from his seat. "No worries, son."

"Dad, sit." Holly glared at her father before jumping from her seat to help him once she realized he wasn't going to listen to her.

She was rewarded with a glare of his own, directed at her. "Who is the parent here, young lady?"

At her father's attitude—which Holly knew was warranted when it came to his pain and disabilities—she couldn't stop her agitation. She only wanted him to take it easy. Before she could register what she was doing, she blurted, "Technically all of us." She placed one of her hands on her stomach and the other on her hip in defiance.

Henry froze with his eyes widened in shock. "Come again?"

"That's one way to tell him," Ben remarked, walking fully into the living room shaking his head. "That's why we wanted to have dinner with you tonight, Henry." Ben darted his eyes to Holly. "Although, we wanted to tell you in a more thought out way."

"Hey, he asked a question and I answered it." Holly moved the hand on her stomach to her other hip narrowing her eyes at Ben.

You wanna fight, Bub. We'll fight.

"Pumpkin?"

Henry's voice brought her attention back to her dad. When she noticed his unsureness, her heart softened. She took a few steps over to him before she wrapped her arms around his waist being mindful of his left side. "You're no longer going to be a grandpa just to the animals."

"You two are having a baby?" he choked out.

Henry squeezed her the best he could before she pulled out of his arms and walked over to Ben's side. She placed her hand on her stomach. "Yes, Dad, we're having a baby."

"We just found out," Ben quietly said into the room as he gave Holly a kiss on her temple before turning his attention back to Henry. "You're finally gonna be a grandpa to human children."

"It's true. Ben took me to the clinic to use his ultrasound thingy and there weren't any horns or anything weird growing," Holly stated.

Henry stared at them not moving.

Then he did what Holly could only assume was a jig, well maybe. He stomped his right foot, and slapped his thigh with his working arm, while a giant lopsided smile appeared on his face. "Hot damn! It's about time!" He started limping their way before bringing them into a hug. "This is wonderful news. No wonder you've been so busy."

Waffles started crying at their feet demanding for him to be the center of attention.

Henry bent at the waist before scratching Waffles behind the ear. "None of that young man. You're gonna be a big brother now. You and your sister are gonna have to protect this little one like your life depended on it. That's your job now."

Waffles cocked his head to the side watching him. "Okay, fine. Like getting a piece of steak depended on it."

Waffles must have registered that since he yipped before his tongue fell out of his mouth.

Holly was pretty sure in Waffles' brain he only heard the word steak and assumed that's what he was getting for dinner. But hey, there was no harm in pretending Waffles realized his new role in the family and showed his excitement.

A mother could only hope, right?

However, the second Waffles looked toward the kitchen and barked, Holly rolled her eyes. *Nope, he thinks he's getting steak.*

"Congratulations, you two!" Henry pulled them in for another hug.

"Love you, Dad."

"Love you too, Pumpkin." Henry started walking toward the kitchen with a pep in his step. "Now, let's eat."

Waffles and Ripley were right behind him.

A chuckle emanated from Ben as he squeezed her into his side. "That was one way to tell him."

Holly shrugged as she pulled out of his arms following her father to the kitchen. They could talk about it later. Right now, it was lasagna time.

As soon as the smell of it hit her nose her mouth watered. Which still blew her mind, before today she wasn't a big fan of it. Now, though, if someone dared to get in between her and the lasagna, she'd murder them with zero remorse.

Holly ran to the food grabbing a fork out of the nearby drawer. She waited impatiently bouncing on her feet as Ben placed the lasagna on top of the stove. As soon as he let go, Holly pushed him out of the way taking a forkful and throwing it into her mouth.

She must have forgotten food that came out of the oven needed to cool. "Hot. Hot. Hot." She did that whole breathing in and out thing, trying to gasp air like she was dying.

"Get used to it, son," Henry said from behind them. "Helen did that exact same thing when she was pregnant."

Ben burst out into a deep laugh as he reached for three plates. He then lightly pushed Holly out of the way with a bump of his hip causing an angry growl to escape from her. *My food.*

"Down, Grace." Ben handed her the first plate.

Seeing the steaming food sent a new wave of cravings through her. It didn't matter she'd burned all her taste buds. It was as if the room faded away and all she saw was the lasagna. She happily took the delicious food as she walked to the kitchen table and plopped down before digging in.

It was like everything faded around her.

She didn't know if it had been three seconds or an hour, but by the time she looked back up, Henry and Ben were lightly chatting about the baby with empty plates in front of them.

"You've finally decided to join the land of the living again there, Pumpkin?" Henry asked with his lopsided grin fully on display.

What just happened?

"Yeah," Ben remarked. "When I asked if you wanted seconds, and went to grab your plate you tried to bite me." Ben's eyes danced with amusement. "I decided it was safer to dump my portion on yours."

Holly sat back in awe. "I have no idea what you're talking about."

"It must be in the genes," Henry laughed.

"I remember when Helen was about four months pregnant, she had an overwhelming craving for peanut butter cake. I had to have the bakery specially make it for her. When I went to pick it up, Helen demanded to come along for the ride. All I can say is that cake never made it home."

"Wait!" Holly threw her arms at her side with a pout. "Now, I want a peanut butter glazed donut."

"Then I'm glad I picked some up before I got here." Ben retrieved the bag he brought into the house. As he handed them to Holly, her heart filled with happiness.

What a perfect man.

Holly looked down at her belly as she retrieved her first donut. *You, little peanut, are gonna have to chill on this blackout eating thing. No one wants a million-pound momma.*

As Holly munched on her food, she idly listened to Ben and her father's chat.

The moment Ben brought up the break-in, however, the image of Jimmy once again flooded her mind.

There was something about that little boy that called to her. She had no idea what it was, but it was there. And it was getting stronger.

The second Holly placed her hand on her stomach, a new image hit her so hard she thought she might vomit.

Jimmy. It was unmistakable. Jimmy with them. All of them, her, Ben, Henry, all their animals. Everyone.

Holly closed her eyes trying and failing to control her breathing as her heart pounded in her chest.

Oh. My. God.

Before she knew what she was doing, she looked up at Ben, her eyes filled with tears. "I want Jimmy."

Chapter Fifteen

WHAT DID SHE SAY?

Ben froze as soon as the words were out of Holly's mouth. It was like in an instant the world had stopped around him. Taking a chance, he looked at his wife.

Her eyes were large, and her mouth open.

Ben's heart started to race as his breathing picked up.

"Did I say that out loud?" Holly rushed out in a panic. "I guess I must have because I'm hearing myself, like for real for real, and not just that voice thing in my head. Right?" Holly started to blink rapidly as she nibbled on her bottom lip like she was working out a problem in her head. "Am I crazy?"

As much as Ben wanted to speak he couldn't. He was still trying to piece together what was going on, so his mouth just opened and closed.

"I feel like I sound crazy," Holly continued. "But now that I said it out loud I can't stop thinking about it. The Universe works in all those weird ways and stuff. What if all this happened just so we could meet Jimmy?" Her eyes pleaded with him, as her words registered to his ears. "See, I am crazy. I don't even know what I'm talking about." Holly placed her

127

head in her hands defeated. "Who thinks like this? And why can't I get his face out of my mind? I don't know what it is, but I have this overwhelming feeling about him being with us."

Holly moved her gaze to Ben. That's when he saw the tears in her eyes. He felt the same, he just didn't know it was possible for Holly to feel it too.

"Ben, I don't know what's wrong with me."

"Nothing." Ben grabbed Holly's hand squeezing it. "Nothing is wrong with you." He looked into her eyes. "I can't explain it either, but I feel the same thing. I haven't stopped thinking about it. I don't know where it came from, it just appeared."

"Can we back up here a moment?" Henry asked, drawing Ben's attention back to him. "Who is Jimmy?"

Where do we even begin?

"Remember I was telling you about the break-in and the information the detective gave us?" Holly answered.

"Yes, the boy who hurt Twitch."

Ben gave Holly's hand another squeeze before he spoke, "There was another boy there."

Henry's face scrunched like he was trying to figure out a problem.

"Will, the detective," Ben continued. "Showed us the surveillance video from that night. Outside of the clinic there was another child, however this one just stood there."

"I—I," Holly blurted. "I can't stop thinking about him."

Ben darted his eyes to Holly. Her panicked face as she worried her bottom lip, had him in awe. He couldn't quite believe that somehow, they were thinking the same thing. If that wasn't the universe at work then what was? He turned back to Henry. "The detective told us the little boy's name was Jimmy. Right now, he currently resides in the foster care system after both of his parents were killed in a car accident."

Henry tilted his head to the side as he stared at them.

"Dad, if you saw the look on his face, you'd understand. There was so much pain, worry, and on top of all that. He was scared."

"And you know all of this, how?"

"Will," Ben stated. "The detective assigned to the case also happens to be a friend of mine. He was probably giving us a little more information than we deserved, but he was telling us why they hadn't moved along with the case."

Ben shot his attention back to Holly. This *did* sound insane when he said it out loud.

Right now, they should be focusing their full attention on the baby they were about to bring into this world. That's what they *should* be doing. That's what any expecting parent would be doing. He knew that.

But then...

"Now hold on here," Henry remarked. "Let me see if I've got this straight. A few days ago, you were introduced to a troubled young boy who helped an older boy break into your veterinarian clinic to *seek revenge*, right?"

"Uhh, yeah."

"Somehow through all this chaos, you both had the same overwhelming feeling about this other youngster. Even with Holly now having a baby. Mind you, a baby you all just found out about."

"Well, when you put it that way..." Holly slumped into her chair.

"I wasn't finished, young lady." Henry gave her a pointed look before turning his attention to Ben. "Now, I can't quite say what is going on in either of your minds. Honestly, I gave up trying to figure Holly out years ago."

"Hey!"

"But, like I've told you in the past, Ben. You don't question yourself or your instincts. You never know what tomorrow will bring. Son, do you remember the conversation we had on the porch the night I met you, about Holly?"

"What conversation? Why am I only hearing about this now?" Holly sat straighter in her seat glaring at her father and Ben.

Ben ignored Holly, as the words Henry had said ran through his mind. "Take that leap and follow your impulse."

"That's right. You said you knew the moment you met Holly she was the one for you. I felt the same way about Helen. People said we were crazy getting married so soon after meeting. People said I was making the biggest mistake in my life. But they were wrong. Even though the years I had with her were cut short, they were the best years of my life." He looked Ben in the eyes. "Sometimes the world works in strange ways. How else could you explain the chance meeting you had here with my little girl?"

"Yeah, still kinda angry about the hit to the face," Holly chimed in causing Henry to chuckle.

"And yet, without that you wouldn't be here right now at my kitchen table talking about a poor child that's lost everything."

Ben sat back trying to digest the words Henry said. He was right, look at how he met Holly. That was a once in a lifetime chance encounter. Ben was just lucky enough that everything aligned correctly and over a year later here he was, with Holly as his wife, who also happened to be carrying his child.

"Maybe my brain is all wonky since finding out about Peanut and I somehow made Ben's brain wonky too." Holly started to worry her hands in defeat.

"No, wait." Ben grabbed Holly's attention. More than ever before Henry's words registered with him. "Let's talk this out. We are having a baby, right?"

"Yes." Holly cocked her brow. "That's been established. Did you see how much food I just ate?"

Ben sent her a warning growl.

"You can't get all growly at me when I state a fact, mister."

Give me strength. Ben took a deep breath ignoring her. "We're both excited about having this baby, right?"

"Again, yes."

When it came to Holly, things were never simple. With a quick roll of his eyes, Ben focused all his attention on his wife. "Holly, without even knowing it, we *both* had this feeling about Jimmy. Something resonated in us when he looked into the camera."

"Well, yeah."

"That has to mean something. You're not crazy. I'm not crazy. And there is one thing I know for sure. Your dad's right, we never know what tomorrow will bring."

"What about Peanut?" Holly placed her hand on her stomach.

"What *about* Peanut?" Ben countered. "We can't deny there is enough love in both of us to give. From day one nothing has ever been normal for us, Grace. Why would we expect this to be any different? What's the harm in figuring out if we would even be suitable for Jimmy?"

The idea of fostering him with the potential of adoption later on, sounded better and better to Ben as the moments ticked on.

I refuse to live my life with regrets. I wouldn't when it came to Holly and I won't now.

Holly slumped back into her chair before placing both of her hands on her stomach in a dramatic show. "Great, now I've got heartburn again."

"That might have to do with what you stuffed into your mouth," Henry laughed, nodding his head to her plate which still housed the last piece of her donut.

Ben bit back his laugh at Holly's glare.

"No," Holly countered. "I'm blaming it on Peanut. This little thing in here is gonna drive me bonkers."

"Why do you keep calling it peanut?" Henry asked.

"That's 'cause Holly can't stop eating peanut butter glazed donuts, so we figured peanut was fitting."

Henry laughed. "That sounds like logic to me."

"Can we stop making fun of me?" Holly pushed out her bottom lip.

"But what would we do with our time, then?" Henry's eyes sparkled as he riled his daughter.

Henry always knew how to lighten the mood.

"Your dad does have a point." Ben sent Holly a wink causing her to growl.

"Whatever." Holly popped the last piece of donut into her mouth.

"Like I said before, you're gonna need to get used to this, son. If Holly is anything like her mother was when she was pregnant with her, you've got a whirlwind ahead of you."

Ben's face brightened as he beamed at his wife. "I'm looking forward to it."

"I'm not going to forget this." Holly glared at them.

After a small chuckle, the room fell into silence as everyone contemplated their discussion. Ben looked back at Holly who was once again worrying her bottom lip.

If anyone could do this, it would be them. He knew that in his heart. And just because they were even thinking about looking into the next steps with Jimmy, didn't mean they would love peanut any less. On the contrary, they both had so much love to give. He planned on having as many children as she'd let him have. He knew this was meant for them.

"What do we do now?" Holly asked, breaking the silence.

"If you want my opinion," Henry started. "I'm going to suggest taking the next few days to really think about this. I don't know much about this process, but I do believe there is a great deal—from fostering to social workers and everything in between. You two are going through a lot of life changes at this exact moment and you want to make the right choices for your growing family."

"You're right," Ben agreed.

"Raising a child is one of the most rewarding things anyone can do. I didn't know what real love was until Holly was born." He looked at both of them. "I would have given anything to have had more children."

Ben sat back staring at Henry as he continued. "Mine or through adoption."

Chapter Sixteen

IT HAD BEEN a total of two weeks since the evening at Henry's house and during that time Holly's feelings about Jimmy had only grown stronger. After that night, Ben and Holly had a serious conversation. One that lasted two days about what they were thinking. There were many back-and-forths, but in the end, they always ended on one conclusion.

They would regret it if they didn't at least try.

The next day Ben called Will.

At first, Will thought they were absolutely insane, but after explaining everything, he soon gave in and got in touch with Jimmy's social worker on their behalf.

Ben had worked tirelessly with his lawyers on the next steps they needed to take.

Holly was still blown away at the fact, if you had money to throw at it, anything could be done. Anyone that said differently was dead wrong.

Not that Ben ever used his money to his advantage, on the contrary, most of the time he gave his share from Richman Industries to local charities around the city, plus, Holly lost track of the number of dog parks around the city that were donated in Ben's name.

And as it turned out, if you had the funds, you could have all the paperwork sent up the chain of command in no time.

That lead us all to this exact moment.

This was going to be their first time meeting Jimmy.

After much deliberation, they decided on going to the dog park. The exact one where Holly and Ben met.

Seemed kind of fitting, if you asked them.

As Ben and Holly sat on the park bench waiting for Jimmy and his social worker to arrive, Holly pulled out the ultrasound photo she carried in her purse from her recent doctor's visit. As she looked down at their peanut, her heart did this flippy thing.

This was her child.

Her and Ben's child.

She didn't know it was possible to love someone before you meet them, but here she was. She was madly in love with Peanut.

Ben put his arm around her shoulders bringing her closer to him. "I still can't believe we are having a baby," he whispered.

"Me too." She kept looking at the photo. "No matter what happens here today, this is our little peanut."

Ben kissed the top of her forehead. "You're right, no matter what happens this is our little one." They both looked at the photo in silence.

"Do you think we're doing a disservice to the baby?" Holly asked. What if bringing Jimmy into their family wasn't right? What if Peanut resented it? Holly knew she had enough love inside of her to love both, but it was insane to be pregnant and also look into fostering another child.

"We've gone over this, Grace." He pulled her closer into

his arms. "Don't second-guess yourself now. Remember, we are going to take this one step at a time."

"You're right," she sighed, leaning into his body.

"First things first. We meet Jimmy and see where it goes from there."

Holly looked at the ultrasound photo once more.

I love you, Peanut. I promise no matter what happens today, that doesn't change. She bit her bottom lip. *I'll do everything I can to make you proud and make the best possible choices I can.*

"They're here," Ben announced, distracting Holly from her thoughts. She looked up to see Jimmy and his social worker making their way toward them.

This was it.

Ben held Waffles and Ripley at his side tightly, as they both stood.

Holly stared at the little brown-haired boy, with the pale skin and expressive eyes, as he came closer to them. She couldn't help that her heart started to flutter.

"Good afternoon," Jimmy's social worker remarked. "I'm Carol, it's nice to finally meet you in person."

"Likewise." Holly reached out her hand to shake Carol's. "I'm Holly."

"And I'm Ben." Ben shook her hand as well, before dropping to his knee in front of Jimmy making them eye level. "Hey, there little guy. I'm Ben."

Jimmy stepped back hiding behind Carol.

"Would you like to meet our dogs?" Ben looked to Carol who nodded.

"This is Ripley," he introduced her, before bringing Waffles to his side. "And this loaf of bread is Lord Waffles."

Jimmy laughed and emerged from behind Carol. "That's a weird name."

"I agree." Ben smiled at him. "He thinks he's the ruler of the world, it's why we call him Lord."

"What about Waffles?"

"I love waffles." Holly rubbed her hand on her stomach. "Yum."

"Really?" Jimmy's face brightened. "Me too!"

"I make some amazing waffles," Ben added.

"You do?" Jimmy's eyes widened as he looked at Ben. "My mom used to make really good waffles."

"I bet they were delicious." The left side of Ben's mouth turned up as he looked at the child as Jimmy moved his attention to Holly. "Do you make waffles?"

"You don't want her waffles, kiddo." Ben looked at Holly with a smirk. "Unless you want burnt, tasteless, rock hard waffles that is."

Jimmy giggled causing Holly's heart to flip again.

"Hey, I did just fine before you." Holly turned her attention to Ben as she glared at him.

"Yes, throwing pre-made waffles in the microwave is the only way to eat them."

"Eww." Jimmy scrunched his nose.

"I agree, kid."

Jimmy looked at Ben and scrutinized the way he was on his left knee. To Holly's surprise, Jimmy then mimicked him. "Can I pet them?" Jimmy asked, checking once again to make sure he looked just like Ben did.

My heart.

"Of course, you can." Ben didn't have to encourage the dogs to go to Jimmy at all. The moment Waffles heard the word 'pet' he was rolling onto his back demanding scratches.

"He's funny."

"You ain't seen nothing yet." Ben looked Jimmy in the eyes. "Would you be okay if I remove their leashes? Then you can run around and play in the park with them."

"Really?" Jimmy's face glowed with childlike excitement.

"Absolutely, squirt." Ben unhooked their collars. In an

instant Ripley took off into the field. Then Waffles flipped onto his feet and nudged Jimmy at his ankles trying to get him to run after Ripley. Jimmy must have understood. Without even a second thought, all three of them were all running around in circles.

Ben stood beside Holly after placing the leashes in his back pocket.

For a few moments everyone watched the sight before them. Holly's heart once again did that thing.

A huge smile appeared on Holly's face as the picture morphed in front of her. However, this time, it had little Peanut playing along with them too.

"I HAVE TO SAY, this is extremely unconventional," Carol remarked, drawing Ben's attention away from Jimmy and the dogs playing.

"We've never been conventional."

"If it weren't for Detective Bower's insistence on this meeting, I wouldn't have allowed it." Carol turned to Ben. "He swore on his career you two were meant for this."

Ben didn't know what to say. He was glad Will stuck his neck out for them, he'd never be able to repay him.

"We appreciate you taking a chance on us," Holly said, saving him from answering.

"Jimmy was afraid to come here today."

"Why?"

"He thought you wanted to punish him since he was there during the break-in."

"We would never," Holly answered appalled.

"Nonetheless, I reassured him you two only wanted to meet him. He only agreed after I told him we were meeting at a dog park."

Thank God we chose this place.

"I've looked into both of your backgrounds, Mr. and Mrs. Richman. I have to say, I was looking for something that would stop this meeting," she was honest. "I don't believe in someone swooping in. These are very young children, impressionable children. Children that sometimes have had their world as they know it ripped from them in an instant. However, there was nothing concerning on either one of you. On the contrary, you both have done so much for the community. I couldn't help but wonder. Especially, you Doctor Richman."

"Please call me Ben."

"Fine, Ben. You donate to local charities every month, you make sure your family's business is being run properly, and you clearly have the funds to sustain fostering a child." Carol looked out to the field. "You need to understand I take my job very seriously. Sometimes I'm all these kids have."

"I'm glad you do."

"Today's meeting is about compatibility," she continued.

Holly bounced on her feet as she looked at the social worker. "Uhh, we want to be honest with you. I'm three months pregnant."

Carol smiled warmly at her. "I was hoping you'd tell me."

"You already knew?"

"Of course, I did. Like I said, I take my job very seriously. I called Detective Bower as soon as I found out to see if this would be something you could handle along with the trials and tribulations of raising a newborn."

"We were made for this," Holly announced proudly.

"That's what Detective Bower said."

They all fell silent as they watched the little boy and dogs play.

"Jimmy's had a hard life," Carol spoke. "No one at his age should have to experience the kind of loss he has. However, to try and cope with his feelings he started turning down the wrong path. His current foster parents don't know what to do with him. That night at the clinic wasn't the first time he'd snuck out of his room."

"He's lost," Ben answered. Even though Ben was much older than Jimmy when his father passed away, he felt the same way. There would be no telling what Ben would have done if it had happened when he was Jimmy's age.

"He is. It's why we're here. At first, I was apprehensive about this, but the more and more I looked into you both I knew he needed to meet you. Call it a weird hunch."

"It's the Universe. It works in weird ways." Holly smiled brightly as she placed her hand on her stomach.

"That it does." Carol turned her attention to Ben. "Mr. Richman, I know your lawyers have been working to file the paperwork, along with that, I will need to check your home and have a few more supervised meetings with the three of you. Do you have any problems with that?"

"Not at all," Holly chimed in. "Our house is pretty much accident proof. It has to be with me around."

"I beg your pardon?"

"What Holly's trying to say is she's the world's champion of tripping over thin air."

Carol laughed. "Huh, I have a daughter like that."

"Then you understand," Ben chuckled. "Our house is as accident proof as it's ever going to get."

Carol nodded.

"It's true." Holly rolled her eyes. "After we found out we were having a baby he bought an industrial size roll of bubble wrap."

"To do what with?"

"Wrap me in it."

Carol laughed at Holly's glare at him.

Ben was sure Holly was remembering when it arrived. It

wasn't his fault Holly wasn't a fan of being wrapped head to toe in bubble wrap. It was a necessity in his eyes. But after a few minutes of wrestling her into the bubble wrap and her then demanding she had to pee he ended up cutting her out of it.

It was definitely a sight to see.

Ben scratched his chin. He was still contemplating a way for her to be wrapped in it when he wasn't around to keep her safe. And he'd figure out a way. He just needed time.

"You seem like a fun pair."

"We're all right," Ben responded with a laugh.

They all idly talked for the next twenty minutes as they watched Jimmy play with the dogs.

However, the moment Holly started ruffling with her bag, Waffles' ears perked up. As if he were in a high-speed chase, Waffles ran to Holly plopping onto his butt in front of her.

"Okay fine, you've been good, so you get a treat. But, listen here, Bub, just 'cause you hear me go in my bag does not mean treat time."

Jimmy laughed as Waffles caught the treat in his mouth. Ripley then barked signaling her treat was needed as well.

"You too, missy." Holly tossed Ripley a treat which she gladly chomped down on.

"When can I play with Waffles again?" Jimmy asked, scratching Waffles' back as his tongue hung out of the side of his mouth. "I really like him. I've always wanted a dog. Mom and Dad said when I was older, they would think about it." Jimmy looked back at Waffles. "I'm older now."

Ripley sensing Jimmy's discomfort nudged her head under his hand, pushing Waffles out of the way. "I like this one too," Jimmy announced, moving to scratch Ripley instead.

Waffles being offended at his scratches being cut in half jumped onto his feet and barked at Ripley. Ripley then turned her back effectively blocking his way to Jimmy.

A smile appeared on Ben's face. He guessed their dogs were now going to fight for Jimmy's attention. "Looks like they both like you too," Ben remarked.

Out of nowhere he could sense Holly was only a few seconds from crying, whether it was the overwhelming feeling of the situation at hand or maybe it had to do with Peanut, he wasn't one hundred percent sure. Regardless, he wrapped his arm around Holly's shoulders pulling her in close.

Then as if Waffles knew they needed the tension to be broken, or he just needed to be the center of attention again... probably the latter. He took a step back then ran full speed at Jimmy knocking him backward onto the grass and started giving him tons of kisses. Ripley not to be outdone started doing the same.

Jimmy's laugh erupted around them.

Waffles nudged at Ripley trying to get her to move out of his way. Ripley then ran toward the open field with Waffles right on her tail.

Surprisingly enough, Jimmy jumped up and ran right after them as his laughter filled the air.

"Looks like they'll be tired out tonight," Ben joked.

"Good. Plus, Waffles needs the exercise," Holly said with a gleam in her eye.

"I must say," Carol interrupted them. "I've been with Jimmy since he was first placed into the system. I've never seen him smile. Not once. Even his foster parents mentioned his lack of joy when doing routine evaluations. All he's done here is smile."

Holly turned to Ben. Her face glowed as her smile spread from ear to ear. "It's Waffles. He does that to everyone."

Carol returned her smile as she wrote something on her clipboard. She then looked at her watch. "Unfortunately, our time here has to come to an end." Carol looked toward the field. "Jimmy, it's time to go!"

Jimmy stopped running after the dogs as a sad expression replaced the smile he had moments ago. He slowly started walking their way with Waffles and Ripley running around him in circles trying to get him to play. When Jimmy made it back to them, he looked up at Ben and Holly, the exact same pain they saw in the video was back in his eyes.

Holly did exactly what Ben had the urge to do. She pulled Jimmy into her arms squeezing him like her life depended on it. "This isn't goodbye, Jimmy."

"It isn't?"

Holly pulled out of their hug but kept her hands on Jimmy's shoulders. "No, buddy, this is a, 'we'll see you real soon.'"

Jimmy then looked to Ben, his eyes wide and hopeful. "Do you promise?"

At that exact moment, Ben's heart soared. He didn't care what he needed to do, or who he needed to get in contact with, but he was damn sure they would keep their promise to Jimmy. Their encounter today only proved what he knew in his heart all along.

Jimmy was made to be in their family.

"I promise."

A wide smile appeared on Jimmy's face as Carol took over and ushered him away. Once he got a few feet from them, he turned back and waved.

Holly and Ben both stood there in silence as they watched Jimmy and Carol leave. When the two were fully out of sight Holly turned to Ben. "He's ours."

Ben agreed.

He kissed the top of her head. Words wouldn't work right now, not even if he tried.

He'd only felt this overwhelming feeling of rightness once in his life before, and that's when he met Holly.

Chapter Seventeen

THE PAST FEW days had been a whirlwind for Ben and Holly. Since meeting Jimmy, they knew they wanted to continue with whatever they needed to do to have him in their lives. Even with Peanut coming they never felt more right about anything.

Ben and Holly walked up the steps to their house with massive grins on their faces. They'd just left his lawyer's office where he signed the last few forms to get the ball rolling to start the process.

"I cannot believe we're doing this," Holly said as they walked through the front door.

"I can," he answered.

Ben followed Holly into the living room where Twitch ran from the back room to greet them. "Hey, little guy."

Twitch started purring as Ben scratched behind his ears. Feeling Twitch's head movement in the palm of his hand reminded him of what they were still dealing with.

Even though they were beyond thrilled with what had started to transpire with Jimmy, they needed to remember there was still a possible threat.

Ben hadn't heard anything from Will since the meeting in his office about the case.

Thankfully, there hadn't been any more occurrences. Ben was hoping everything had died down, and the kid had given up or at least felt he got his revenge. And after talking with Carol the other night there hadn't been any threats to Jimmy.

Which was a good thing.

A wave of protectiveness rushed through Ben. He would stop at nothing to protect Jimmy. He wasn't surprised at that feeling, though. Since meeting Jimmy, in Ben's mind he was already theirs. Right now, they were just crossing all the T's and dotting all the I's as far as he was concerned.

As Ben placed Twitch on the floor his phone rang. Quickly he retrieved it. "Speak of the devil. Hey, Will, how's it going?"

"Great," he answered. *"I have good news."*

Ben looked at Holly who was staring at him with her brow arched. "Oh, yeah. What's that?"

"Four days ago, we located and detained the suspect. He's since confessed. It didn't take long for him to admit everything. You don't need to worry anymore, this time he's being sent to a rehab facility in hopes to get him the help he needs."

There was a wave of relief that washed through Ben. "You're kidding me?"

Holly started mouthing 'what' as she flung her arms around trying to get Ben's attention.

"I'm not. I would have called sooner but with everything happening, I couldn't."

"Seriously, this is great news, Will. And, don't worry about it. We've been kind of busy ourselves."

Holly picked up a pen from the coffee table and threw it at him. When he ducked out of the way she narrowed her eyes.

"I can imagine with the baby coming and then the meeting with Jimmy and his social worker. How did that go?"

A bright smile appeared on Ben's face. "Really well. Actually, better than well. It was amazing."

"I'm glad to hear that." Ben could hear papers being shuffled around. *"Okay, well, I got to go. Paperwork won't fill out itself, you know? You'll have to call me in a few days so we can catch up on how the meeting went. Martha is dying to have you and Holly over."*

"Of course." Ben smiled at Holly who was now threatening to throw a book at him. "Hey, Will, wait a second."

"Yeah."

There was something inside of Ben that told him he needed to do more. He avoided the book Holly tossed perfectly at his head, as he spoke, "Can you send the info of the rehab facility to my lawyers?"

"Why?"

"What in the hell is going on?" Holly growled at Ben, which had him holding up his hand to her.

"I'd like to offer some financial assistance." Ben watched as Holly's eyes widened. "What?" she whispered.

The other line of the phone was silent. "Will, you there?"

"Yeah, yeah, I'm here," he answered. *"I'm a little in shock. I guess I just forgot how truly good of a guy you are."*

"Everyone deserves a second chance in life. And if going to rehab can help this kid then I want to be a part of it. It's what my dad would have done." That's exactly what his dad would have done, Ben knew that. He always told him, desperate people make desperate choices. You never know what a second chance could give them.

"I'll take care of it."

"Thanks, Will. I'll call you in a few days." Ben ended the call smiling at his wife. Things were looking up.

"What's going on?"

"They arrested the kid that broke into the clinic."

"They did?" Holly's eyes widened.

"Yeah, he's being sent to a rehabilitation center. I want to offer some financial assistance to him."

"Whoa."

Ben shrugged at Holly's shocked expression.

"I really did marry the best guy ever." Holly smiled brightly. "After what he did to Twitch I would have told them to throw away the key."

"You did." Ben pulled her into his arms kissing the top of her head. He ignored her other statement. He got it, Holly loved Twitch with everything inside of her. But he knew he needed to do this.

"I really did, though." Holly wrapped her arms around him. "After having lunch with Emma yesterday, I've realized more and more what a jackpot I got in you hitting me in the face."

"I didn't hit you in the face."

"The Frisbee *you* threw hit me in the face." She shrugged. "Same difference."

"I told you to watch out."

"And you know now how fast I am at reacting."

"How was I supposed to know that?"

Holly reached up on her toes and kissed his nose. "You're right, you wouldn't." Holly pulled out of his grasp as she walked out of the room shaking her ass.

"Oh, you are gonna get it." Ben ran after her scooping her into his arms as he rushed them both to the bedroom.

"Hey, hey, hey now, precious cargo here." She placed her hand on her stomach.

"You've always been." He leaned over capturing his lips with hers. "I love you, Holly."

As Ben started kissing along Holly's jawline, she leaned her head back giving him better access.

She couldn't be happier than she was at this exact moment. Things with Jimmy were working out, the clinic situation had been taken care of, and her little peanut was happy and healthy protected inside of her.

She opened her eyes to see Ben looking down at her with the corner of his mouth turned up.

"What's that look for, Mrs. Richman?"

"I'm happy."

"Me too." Ben pulled his shirt over his head tossing it behind him. "And we're about to be much happier."

Holly burst out into giggles.

"Oh, do you think that's funny?" Ben arched his brow at her. "I'll show you funny." He started tickling her causing Holly to thrash around on the bed.

"Stop, stop," she pleaded.

"Not on your life." During the onslaught of tickles, Ben somehow managed to remove Holly's shirt *and* bra.

"How'd you do that so fast?" she asked after realizing she was indeed topless.

"Eye on the prize, babe." He winked.

Holly rolled her eyes. "At least you didn't rip them this time."

"The night's still young." Ben grabbed the waistband of her pants pulling them down her legs exposing her sex.

The way Ben looked at her when she was naked always sent Holly into overdrive. Every person deserved someone that looked at them like this. Ben's eyes held so much passion and desire, it drove her fucking wild.

Ben reached around her grabbing one of their pillows. "Over," he demanded. He flipped Holly onto her stomach taking the pillow he'd grabbed propping it under her hips.

Holly looked at him from over her shoulder. "What about you? You've still got your clothes on."

"Not for much longer." Ben unbuckled his pants before jumping from the bed and tossing them to the side.

"That's better." Holly wiggled her ass in the air. She loved this. So, fucking much.

Nothing could stop them when they got to this point.

However, just as Ben hopped back on the bed Holly heard a bark.

Ben sighed loudly. "I forgot to shut the door."

This caused Holly to burst into laughter. "You might as well get used to the interruptions," she said. "Soon, there's gonna be more than just us in the house."

"No," Ben growled. "I'm just gonna have to remind myself to close the door." Ben grabbed his pair of boxers tossing them all around in the air getting the dogs' attention before throwing them out into the hall.

Holly had to bite her lip when she saw Twitch run after the dogs a few seconds later, once he realized they were now going after the piece of clothing instead of them.

Once the door was shut Ben crawled back onto the bed. "Now, where were we?"

Holly pushed her ass into the air.

"Oh, that's right." Ben got behind her before bending to kiss her exposed back.

"While we have the house to ourselves, we might as well make the best of it."

"Huh?" she said, looking over her shoulder at him confused.

He gave her a wicked grin before entering her in one fast movement causing her to moan loudly.

"Loud, Grace. I want to hear you scream my name."

She sent him back a grin that matched his. She pushed her ass making him enter her deeper. "My pleasure."

Chapter Eighteen

TWO MONTHS LATER

Today was the day.

And, not just any day, this was *the day*. Everything Ben and Holly had worked toward was finally coming together. And Holly couldn't be more excited.

Today, Jimmy came to live with them.

Of course, his social worker, Carol, would still be making frequent checks, but as of this morning, Jimmy was officially their foster child. It had been two months getting all the foster certifications, and everything else, but all the wait was worth it.

Holy freaking crap on all the crackers!

Holly placed her hand on her growing stomach. Who knew so much could change in the blink of an eye?

Holly looked around their home and sighed. She wanted to pat herself on the back. They'd spent a great deal of time making sure everything was in order. They redecorated one of the guest rooms for Jimmy, which Ben had a blast doing.

Seriously, when they went into their local toy store, Ben's face lit up like he was a kid in a freaking candy shop.

It was cute. A little disturbing, especially when he pouted

after Holly told him to put back a couple of items that were more for *him* than Jimmy. But still cute.

They had everything in place.

But maybe...

Holly jumped from her spot on the couch and ran to the spare bedroom that would now be Jimmy's room. Waffles and Ripley ran alongside her with Twitch trailing them.

Poor little Twitch he was always one step behind.

Once Holly got to the room, she did another once-over.

Bed: check.

Clothes: check.

Toys: double check.

As her eyes scanned the room, she noticed Waffles had moved to the corner. He was on his back already snoozing with his tongue flopped out. Typical Waffles.

That was fast. Wait a second!

"A dog bed!" Holly yelled. "We need a dog bed in here! Why didn't I think of it sooner?" She smacked her forehead with her hand. Once the room was finished, Waffles and Ripley had taken turns with who owned it. Ripley normally won since she easily pushed Waffles out into the hall. It was quite funny to watch them fight over the room.

Holly ran back into the living room where they had an abundance of dog beds that none of the dogs used—since they'd rather sleep on the couch—and brought one of the beds back into Jimmy's room.

After she placed it in the corner, she sighed in relief. "Crisis averted."

Then her eyes shot open. "The nursery!"

Holly ran into her and Ben's room grabbing the expensive dog bed they bought a few months ago that was only ever used by Twitch, and brought it to the nursery.

Holly placed the bed in the opposite corner of the crib. Proud of herself, she stood in the middle of the room and looked around. Holly then smacked her forehead with her hand. "Why in the hell did I just do that?"

The nursery was nowhere close to being done. And now, in a disheveled room there was a dog bed just chilling on the floor. "I need to get a grip."

As if Waffles wanted to agree with her, he barked.

"Thanks, Bub."

Waffles barked again.

Deciding to ignore him, she went back into the living room to wait patiently. *Why in the hell am I all over the place?*

Oh yeah, that's right, her and Ben were about to bring a child into their home.

Holy crap.

This was real.

Holy. Freaking. Crap.

Holly took a deep breath as she sat on the couch. This was it. There was no going back now. She placed her hands on her stomach. "Are you ready for this, Peanut?"

Holly was instantly rewarded with a small bump to her hand. Damn, every time that happened, she still freaked out a little. In a good way, well, after the first few times that is.

I'm gonna take that kick as a yes.

She still couldn't believe there was a baby growing inside of her.

The first time Peanut kicked, Holly thought some part of her body had broken. It wasn't strong, but it was enough to get her attention. And got her attention did it ever.

Holly and Ben were lying in bed when it happened.

At first, Holly could swear her bladder exploded and she'd peed herself. Then after feeling it again, she couldn't stop herself from envisioning an alien creature jumping out of her stomach before doing a tap dance on the bed.

Ben thought it was funny.

Holly not so much.

However, once her irrational fears were gone of being ripped in half, or eaten from the inside out, she loved feeling Peanut, even if it was small little bumps.

So did Mildred.

The old bat would follow Holly around work begging the little one to kick. It was hard to explain to the board of directors the day they came in why a crazy old lady wouldn't let go of Holly's stomach.

Although, as much as Mildred annoyed Holly, she'd really helped her and Ben out. Between Ben's lawyers and Mildred's contacts, they were really able to get everything in order for Jimmy to live with them.

Holy crap, Jimmy was coming today!

There had to be more that she could do. "Maybe he'd want cookies. That's what parents do, right? They make cookies. I can do that." Holly jumped from her seat and ran into the kitchen.

"This can't be so hard." Holly pulled out her phone before searching *easy fast cookie recipes*. Once she found one that only had a few steps she moved around the room searching for the ingredients.

With Waffles, Ripley, and Twitch weaving in between her legs, she did her best to stay focused. Calling the fire department was not on her list of things to do today.

Holly looked down at her fur-babies. "I need you all to simmer down now. Mommy's going to try and bake some cookies."

Ripley and Waffles both cocked their heads.

"Don't give me that look."

Then that dang judgmental dog of hers sent her such a side-eye it almost knocked her on the floor. "Waffles don't you dare judge me. I can do this."

He huffed.

"I can!"

Holly could swear Waffles rose his tiny brows at her. *Well, I'll just show him.* Ignoring her holier than thou dog, Holly turned to the oven and set it to preheat.

Carefully she read the instructions and started placing the ingredients in the bowl. "Softened butter? What the hell is that?" Holly looked at the recipe. "What do you do, sit on it?"

She heard Waffles bark from the other room.

"Stop judging me!"

Waffles barked again.

"No treats for you!" She then heard a dramatic whine. *Serves him right.*

After going back to her recipe, she looked at all the steps involved. This one seems too hard. *Seriously, softened butter was stupid.* Deciding to backtrack she quickly found another recipe with only a few steps.

Perfect.

Looking at her bowl of already mixed ingredients she shrugged. *I'm sure it's close enough.*

This recipe also called for melted butter rather than softened. *That I could do.* She threw the butter in the microwave.

How long do you put butter in for?

Hitting three minutes she waited.

When it hit the thirty-five-second mark the popping started growing louder. Waffles and Ripley followed by Twitch ran into the kitchen to investigate.

As the noise got louder, they started barking and jumping all around the room begging her to do something.

"I know, I know, I don't know what to do!"

It's like bombs were going off in her microwave.

Holly quickly grabbed the lid of a pot and shielded herself as she released the latch opening the microwave door.

"Ahhh!" she screamed as loud as she could as she jumped back hiding her head behind the lid. After a few seconds, the popping subsided so Holly carefully looked past her shield to see the bowl sitting in the microwave as if nothing had happened.

Holly wiped her brow. *See, that wasn't so bad. I could do this all the time*, she thought. *Cookie master, here I come.*

Waffles and Ripley, on the other hand, we're running around like it was World War III. Deciding they were just being overly dramatic, Holly grabbed two potholders and carefully removed the butter and placed it on the counter.

"Damn that's hot." *Of course, it's hot dumdum it nearly exploded in the microwave.*

Once the butter was in the bowl with the other ingredients, Holly gently started mixing. When she read the recipe further it called for baking soda. She looked through their cabinets but came up empty. "That's the same thing as baking powder, right?" *Ehh, it'll be fine.*

Holly finished mixing in the ingredients deciding to forgo the salt too. *Who puts salt in cookies? That sounds horrible.*

She looked down at Waffles who was once again giving her a severe side-eye. "Stop judging me, you judging McJuderson. No one needs your type of negativity in their life."

Holly carefully spooned out droplets and placed them on the cookie sheet.

After they were all on the baking sheet, she took a good look at them and grimaced. They did look a little weird. One of them was even spreading outwardly like a blob trying to eat the other blobs. She shrugged. "I'm sure they'll be fine."

She placed them into the oven and set two timers. One on the stove and one on her phone.

See no fire department this time. I've got this. Call me Chef Holly from now on.

She'd rather not add this to Ben's ever-growing list of incidents with her cooking.

Holly's phone chimed signaling she got a text message. Mindlessly she placed her hand on her stomach as she read it.

BEN

Grace, I'm pulling into your Dad's. We're going to stop at the store and then we'll be home. Don't do anything stupid.

Holly glared at the phone.

HOLLY

Why would I do anything stupid?

BEN

Grace...

Oh, he was going to get it.

HOLLY

Do not Grace me!

BEN

We'll be there soon. Have you heard anything from the social worker?

Before she could respond the doorbell rang. "Oh God, it's happening. It's really happening!"

Holly ran to the front room stumbling over the dogs as they ran next to her. The moment she got to the door she swung it open with her arms held wide to greet them.

"Waffles!" Jimmy ran right past her and straight for the dogs.

"Nice to know up front where I rank on the importance list," she laughed, causing Carol to laugh along with her.

"Don't feel so bad. All Jimmy's talked about since everything finalized was Waffles, Ripley, and Twitch. I guess the times we've come for supervised visits really resonated with him."

Outranked by the pets. "At least we have that going for us." Holly placed her hand on her belly.

"How are you doing?" Carol asked.

"Pretty good. Heartburn makes me pray for death, but other than that I'm good. Still want the donuts, though."

Carol laughed.

"Mrs. Holly, can I go play outside with the dogs?" Jimmy ran to her with his big expressive eyes pleading.

"Call me, Holly, squirt, we've talked about this." Holly softened as she looked at the little brown-haired boy with the green eyes that had captured her heart. "How about we wait for Ben to come home and we can all go outside and play? He'll be here soon."

"Oh, man." Jimmy turned back to the dogs. "Sorry guys."

"Why don't you grab your stuff from the car, and we can put it in your room?"

Jimmy's eyes brightened. "That's right! I get my own room now!"

It was funny how attention spans changed so quickly with kids. Like a flash, he was running to the car grabbing his belongings. It was heartwarming to watch as Waffles and Ripley run along with him as he grabbed his things.

On Jimmy's last visit to the house, they'd shown him where his room was going to be. You'd think the kid had won the lottery or something. Her smile spread from ear to ear as Holly turned to Carol. "Thank you."

"I didn't do anything, Mrs. Richman."

"But you did." Holly's heart pounded in her chest as Carol looked at her with a warm smile.

Life is perfect.

BEN PULLED into the driveway with Henry in the passenger seat. His heart raced and his palms were sweaty.

This is it.

This was their moment.

Ben saw Carol's car parked in front of their house. He knew the second he walked through the front door his life would be forever changed.

"Son, I can't tell if you're excited or gassy," Henry joked.

Ben laughed as he looked at Henry with a smile on his face. "This is it," Ben answered.

"It is. And, how do you feel about that?"

"It's about damn time." Ben jumped out of the car, with pure adrenaline. He felt more excited than ever. He ran around the passenger side and carefully helped Henry out. Sure, he was eager to get through the front door but he knew so was Henry.

Henry hadn't been able to meet Jimmy yet. All of the supervised visits had been conducted at their house.

Ben imagined Henry was just as excited to potentially meet his first grandson as he was to finally have Jimmy home with them.

Once they made it to the front door, Ben pushed it open as his heart slammed against his chest. There in front of him was Jimmy on the floor wrestling with Waffles and Ripley with Twitch jumping on him whenever he got a chance. Then he saw Holly on the couch holding her extended belly. When she caught his eye, she winked before her smile overtook her whole face.

This was home.

"Ben!" Jimmy jumped from his spot on the floor and ran toward Ben wrapping his arms around his waist giving him a tight hug. "Oomph." Fuck, his heart nearly exploded in his chest.

"Hey, little guy!" Ben squeezed him back before rustling his hair. *Yep, this is what could bring a man to his knees.*

"You're here! We can go outside and play with the dogs now!" Jimmy ran toward the back door but Ben stopped him.

"Hold up a second, squirt," he laughed. "I want you to meet someone."

Jimmy moved his focus to Henry. "Hello," he said shyly.

"Hi," Henry answered. Ben could hear the emotions in Henry's voice. "I'm Grandpa Henry."

Jimmy cocked his head to the side. "I've never had a grandpa. Mine died before I was born."

"Well, then." Henry puffed out his chest. "I'm glad I came around."

Jimmy face morphed into a toothy grin.

"I'm Holly's dad."

Jimmy turned to Holly who gave him an encouraging nod. "That's right. He's my dad."

"That's cool!" Jimmy then surprised them all by running to Henry wrapping his arms around his waist. "It's nice to meet you, Grandpa Henry. Can we go play with the dogs now?"

Ben bit back his laugh through his emotions. Leave it to kids to have a one-track mind.

Ben glanced over at his wife. The smile she had on her face melted him.

Yep. This was home.

"Yeah," Henry answered. "I can't play too well with them. See I've got some issues, but I can watch you play along with the pups."

Jimmy gave Henry the once-over assessing him. "That's okay. I can play with them for both of us." Jimmy grabbed Henry's good hand as if he knew, and carefully pulled Henry toward the backdoor.

Holly and Ben stared at them in shock.

Holy shit. Yeah, they wanted Jimmy to feel comfortable with them and Henry, they didn't expect this.

"I have to tell you both, since that first meeting at the dog park, Jimmy has changed considerably. He smiles, he talks nonstop about both of you and the pets." Carol's face softened looking at them. "I know this isn't a done deal yet, but I have to say, I became a social worker for cases like this. The ones where in the end everything falls perfectly into place."

Joy filled the room as Holly moved into Ben's arms. He couldn't agree more.

Then he heard it. It was faint, but he definitely could hear something. "Babe, what's that beeping noise?"

"What beeping noise?"

Ben sniffed the air. "Is something burning?"

"Shit! My cookies!" Holly raced from his arms into the kitchen. Ben saw her glare at the oven timer that was still set to ten minutes. He had to bite his lip to stop from laughing. Clearly, Holly never hit start on her cookies. And seeing that her phone was on the counter, the ringer turned almost all the way down, she didn't stand a chance.

"Oh no!" Holly pulled the cookies out of the oven.

Instantly, his stomach churned. He didn't know cookies could look like that. Wait, she did say they were cookies, right?

"They're ruined!" Holly turned to him, tears in her eyes.

Damn pregnancy hormones. Then again cooking was never her strong suit. Pregnant or not. "No, Grace, they're fine. They are just a little well done."

"Well done? These are beyond well done. They aren't even cookie shape. They're like this big ole blobby thingy." She looked back at him the tears now threatening to escape. "I followed the recipe. I promise... Well, kinda."

"I'm sure they taste fine, Holly." Ben swallowed hard as he looked at the cookie sheet. "Now, don't take this the wrong way, but I have to ask, with your track record what made you want to bake cookies in the first place?"

"That's what moms do! They bake cookies. I wanted to bake Jimmy cookies!" she cried.

"What's all the calliwacking going on in here?" Henry

asked, coming in from the back yard. "We could hear the squawking from all the way out there."

"Holly tried to bake cookies," Ben answered.

"Why would you do something crazy like that?" Henry asked appalled, looking at his daughter. "Wait are those the cookies?" Henry's face morphed into disgust.

"Yes!" Holly growled. *Damn the mood swings are strong.* He placed his hand behind his neck. Did he just get whiplash from that?

"They don't look like any cookies I've ever seen." Henry scrunched his nose.

"Hush your face, old man."

"What did you say, young lady?"

There was that whiplash again. Tears appeared in Holly's eyes as her body deflated. "Sorry, Dad."

"That's more like it."

Jimmy stood beside Henry as he tried to make sense of the situation. He had Twitch in his arms, as they both looked at the pile of cookies.

Henry looked to Ben then back at the cookies. He knew what his father-in-law was suggesting in order to ward off Holly's tears.

One bite, that's all you have to do, Ben told himself. He looked back at Henry, who took a small step back. *What happened to team effort?*

When Ben tried to take a piece of the pile'o'cookie from the sheet, it didn't budge. *Did she use cooking spray?*

Knowing Holly, she probably hadn't.

Fuck.

Ben grabbed a kitchen knife and chiseled out a small piece. He brought it to his mouth before taking a deep breath. *Please don't kill me.* He shoved it in his mouth.

Holy fuck! Nope. Nope. Nope!

He couldn't do it. He spit it out so fast he was sure he'd won a world record.

"Ben!" Holly cried.

"I tried, I really did, babe." Ben used the back of his hand to wipe the god-awful taste out of his mouth. *That's it. Holly is now officially banned from the kitchen.*

Jimmy's laugh brought Ben from his thoughts of death by poisoned cookie. He saw Henry bent whispering something into Jimmy's ear.

Ben was positive it had something to do with *never* eating Holly's cooking.

Good advice if you asked him.

Ben pulled Holly into his arms, but she jumped back glaring at him. He bit back his smile.

Carol laughed. "This is going in the books as one of my best placements."

The corner of Ben's mouth turned up. He agreed.

Waffles trotted into the kitchen cocking his head at Ben, judging.

Don't look at me that way, Bub. I was trying to be nice to your mother.

Ben held up a piece of the whatever the hell this thing was – he refused to call it a cookie, in Waffles' direction. The appall on Waffles' face had Ben laughing.

I'm right there with you, Waffles.

Chapter Nineteen

"WHAT ARE we doing at the police station?" Jimmy asked Ben as they made their way up the steps.

Ben couldn't hide his smirk even if he tried. Although, he was moderately sad he couldn't get John on board for this bonding experience. John had to *arrange some things*. Whatever that meant. John had been strangely absent the past few weeks, but nonetheless, he was excited to finally put his plan into motion. "Let's call it a harmless prank."

Jimmy cocked his head to the side trying to understand Ben's logic. "What does going to the police station have to do with a prank?"

"You've been with us a few days now, so you'll understand when I say Holly overreacts with a dramatic flair."

"Like Lord Waffles."

Ben's grin spread from ear to ear. "Yes, exactly like Lord Waffles."

"So, are we going to prank Holly at the police station?"

Ben looked at Jimmy's curious expression. There was a part of Ben that said not to corrupt little Jimmy, but there was a bigger part of him that screamed pranking Holly was of utmost importance.

A good responsible adult would say forget it and take Jimmy out for some ice cream, but then... ehh, a little adventure never hurt anyone. "Holly got a little, how should I say it... high-strung when she met a particular officer a while back which ended with her in handcuffs and a promise to never go near the officer again."

"Are we going to get her in trouble?"

The concern on Jimmy's face had Ben questioning his decision. "Not really. I'm going to see if that same officer wouldn't mind playing a tiny prank on her. Nothing that will get her in trouble." He hoped, Holly did tend to go half-cocked at times...okay, all the time.

Jimmy stopped walking up the steps as he looked at Ben biting his bottom lip. "What about the baby she's carrying in her belly? Would you be pranking the baby too?"

Whoa, Ben had to take a step back. The concern Jimmy had for their baby had his heart tighten. How could this little boy have gone through so much hurt and still be so caring? Jimmy deserved the world, and even if it was the last thing he did, Ben promised to give it to him. "I'll make sure the officer understands it's just a little prank and not to cause any harm to her or the baby."

"Good!" Jimmy face morphed into joy. "I want to meet Peanut."

Holy shit we hit the jackpot. Ben ruffled his hair. "Me too, squirt."

Ben held the door open letting Jimmy through. "Hi Emma, it's good to see you again." Ben smiled at her as they made their way to the reception desk.

"Doctor Richman!" Emma jumped from her seat startled to see him.

"Ben," he corrected. "How many times do I have to tell you, it's Ben?" Emma's gaze dropped to the ground.

"Hey, it's okay, you're a friend now, Emma. Holly hasn't stopped talking about your lunch dates." He smiled warmly at her.

Panic flashed through Emma's eyes. "Holly talks about me?"

Shit. "Only good stuff," he was quick to add. Holly hadn't gone into much detail about Emma's past, but he knew it wasn't good.

He also knew that John hadn't left Emma alone. He wasn't quite sure if that was a good *or* bad thing? Hell, he and John were shooting some hoops a few weeks ago and Emma was all John could talk about. *"Emma's beautiful... Emma has a strange dog... Emma has these dark brown eyes you can get lost in... Emma this and Emma that."*

He wondered if that's how he sounded when Holly came into his life.

It was nauseating.

But there was something John wasn't letting on to. Every time the word dating came up, or anything about relationships, John would get this stormed look in his eyes.

Ben wanted to know more, but he knew when John was ready to talk, he'd come to him.

"This must be Jimmy," Emma said, changing the subject.

Ben pulled the little boy in front of him. "You'd be correct. Jimmy meet Emma, she's a family friend."

"Hi," Jimmy said as he looked a little unsure at Emma.

"Do you want to know something really cool about her?"

Jimmy snapped his attention back to Ben as he nodded his head excitedly. "Yeah!"

"She has a dog the size of you."

"No way!"

"Yes, way, she has a Great Dane. And he's this tall." Ben held his hand up to show how tall Bruce was.

"That's so cool." Jimmy turned to Emma. "Do you ride him?"

Emma burst into laughter at Jimmy's question. "No, I'm afraid I'd hurt him."

"Why?"

"Uhh…" Emma looked down at her body and then back to Jimmy. She then looked at Ben at a complete loss.

"Sometimes Great Danes can have really bad back problems, squirt," Ben replied.

"Ohh." Jimmy gazed at Ben in wonder. "You know all about animals."

"That's what happens when you become a veterinarian."

Jimmy's next words had Ben's throat tighten. "I want to be a veterinarian just like you when I'm older."

An arrow right through the heart. *Holy shit.*

"That way I can know all about the animals too and take Lord Waffles and Ripley with me to work."

"Ben is the best vet around," Emma chimed in.

"Then I'll be the best vet around too."

Emma smiled warmly at Jimmy. "I bet you will."

"Can I meet your dog?"

Emma looked at Ben. "I'm sure one day we can arrange it."

"You bet, squirt." Ben pulled Jimmy into his arms. There was still so much to learn about him, but there was one thing he knew for certain, Jimmy had a heart of gold. Even after losing his parents and being shuffled around in the foster system.

Jimmy's newfound joy probably had a lot to do with Lord Waffles. Ben smiled.

"What can I do for you two boys?" Emma asked with a

bright smile on her face. "Are you here to see Detective Bower?"

"Not exactly, we are actually here to see Officer Jones if he's around."

Emma gave him a sideways look. "Should I be worried?"

"Not at all." Ben smirked.

"I feel like I should be worried."

"We're going to play a tiny prank on Holly, but not on the baby."

Emma narrowed her eyes at Ben. "Is that so?"

Ben held his hands in surrender. "Nothing too crazy, you know just some good old-fashioned bonding between me and Jimmy."

"Mmhhhmm," Emma said before looking at her computer. Ben was going to have some explaining to do, he could see it now. "Officer Jones actually got in not long ago, he's probably at his desk," Emma remarked still giving him the eye.

Clearly, once you were Emma's friend you were under her protection, and if that look she was giving him said anything, it was he better keep this short and simple or her and Holly were going to murder him.

Good to know.

Ben hurried Jimmy along the way. "Thanks, Emma."

Maybe this was a bad idea.

As they rounded the corner Will appeared. "Ben! It's good to see you. What are you doing here?"

"You too, Will."

"Hey Jimmy, do you remember me?" Will asked, crouching down to get on Jimmy's level.

"Yeah, you were the one that came to ask me all the questions."

"That's right," Will softened. "How are you doing, Jimmy?"

"Did you know Mr. Ben and Mrs. Holly have a dog that thinks he's human? He's so much fun, and then there is Ripley, she's really smart and sleeps with me at my feet every night. Twitch does too because Twitch doesn't leave Ripley's side. Waffles comes in every once in a while, but if I don't pet his belly enough, he gets mad and leaves in a huff. It's a lot of fun. And, I have my own room." He beamed at Will.

"It sounds like you're having a good time."

"The best. I really like living with Mr. Ben and Mrs. Holly."

"We like you living with us too, squirt. But you can just call us Ben and Holly. You know that." Ben crouched pulling him into his arms. Giving him a squeeze. He knew it was hard for him. He hadn't opened up about his parents yet, and Ben suspected it would be some time before he did, but while Jimmy was learning to trust them, he would do whatever he could to make him feel comfortable.

"I know."

Just then Officer Jones walked by. "Exactly the man we came here to see." Ben stood, grabbing Officer Jones's attention.

The officer turned to face them, his brow arched. He looked at Jimmy and then back to Ben. "What can I do for you?"

Ben pulled Jimmy to stand in front of him. "Jimmy and I were wondering if you wouldn't mind helping us play a prank on Holly."

"Just a tiny one and only on Holly, not the baby," Jimmy reiterated.

That got Officer Jones's attention. "You're wife?"

"Yes."

"What kind of prank?" Ben saw Officer Jones's smile start to appear.

"How about we sit down for a few minutes and discuss it?"

A wicked smile formed on the officer's face. "My pleasure." He turned leading Ben and Jimmy to his desk leaving Will shaking his head as he walked into his office.

HOLLY WAS LATE. Super late.

She was supposed to meet Ben and Jimmy at her dad's over thirty minutes ago.

And Holly was blaming her lateness one hundred and twenty percent on Mildred. If the woman hadn't stopped going on and on about babies and then running after her to feel her stomach, she would have gotten her work done in time.

But no, Mildred blocked her path every single step of the way today. If Holly didn't know any better, she would have thought she did it on purpose.

And now... Now, Holly was late and the worst part was Ben had sent her a text letting her know they'd picked up donuts.

So, in the grand scheme of things Mildred stood between her and her delicious donuts. And that wasn't okay.

You don't keep a pregnant woman away from her tasty treats. That was just wrong.

Holly looked in the back seat. She would have already been at her father's if she didn't have to run home and grab his holiness, and Ripley.

God forbid they had dinner at her dad's and the dogs weren't there.

Sure, Jimmy would have been upset but it was the meltdown from her dad she didn't want.

No one denied him his visitation to his grand dogs and lived to see another day.

As Holly saw her father's house come into view, she looked down at her belly. "Peanut, I swear please on all things peanut buttery and delicious, please I beg you, take most of your genes from Ben's side."

That's when she heard the siren and saw the flashing lights out of the corner of her eye.

"You have got to be kidding me!" Could today get any worse? Not in her book. She looked over at her father's house that housed the three men she loved... but more importantly her donuts.

Holly pulled over onto the side of the road directly in front of Henry's house. The moment Waffles realized they were stopped and at grandpa's he started to whine. She narrowed her eyes at him. "Could you not?"

Waffles glared at her, before huffing his response.

Universe, if you have any mercy inside of you, I beg you to take me now. I'm done with today, Holly pleaded as she looked to the roof of her car.

"License and registration, ma'am."

Holly jumped as soon as the all too familiar voice hit her. "Holy fuck!" She turned slowly to see her arch nemesis Officer Jones cocking his brow in her direction over his dark sunglasses. "Excuse me, ma'am?"

"Uh oh," Holly started to stammer.

"License and registration," he said again.

This cannot be happening. Play it cool, Hol, maybe he doesn't remember who I am.

"Threaten anyone lately?" he asked, causing a cold sweat to break out on the back of Holly's neck.

He remembers.

"I'm not sure what you're referring to," she did her best to sound calm as she reached for the glove box.

"I have to ask you to keep your hands where I can see them."

Holly snapped her attention to Officer Jones. "Well how in the hell do you expect me to get you my registration if you won't let me go into the glove box?" Waffles barked from the back. "Exactly!" She caught Waffles' eye in the rearview mirror and nodded at him in solidarity.

"Ma'am, have you been drinking?"

Oh, hell fucking no!

"Have I been drinking?" Holly pointed to her belly. "I'm almost six and a half months pregnant. Do *you think* I've been drinking?"

Cop or not she was going to strangle him. How dare he insinuate she'd be so careless to harm her child? Her blood boiled.

"I'm going to have to ask you to step out of the car, ma'am."

"If I step out of this car it's only gonna be to punch you in your throat."

Officer Jones pushed his sunglasses to the top of his head as he stared her down. "Is that another threat? Are you threatening an officer?"

Holly unbuckled her seatbelt as fast as she could before throwing open the door forcing Officer Jones to take a step back. "It's a promise."

When Holly saw a smirk appear on Officer Jones's face, she cocked her arm back.

"Grace!"

Unfortunately, as she geared up for the hit, the sound of footsteps running in her direction accompanied by Ben's voice distracted her. On her unsteady footing, she turned toward the house too fast.

Before she knew it, she was tumbling over.

Holly couldn't even blame it on her new center of gravity.

Nope.

Look out ground, here I come.

Officer Jones was fast, though. Within seconds he had her in his arms, catching her before anything happened.

"Fuck!" Ben ran to her. "You weren't supposed to get hurt."

"What are you talking about?" Her adrenaline rushed through her.

"And you wonder why I bring up the damn bubble wrap every other day?"

"Benjamin Richman, you are not wrapping me up in that shit. I'd suffocate you with it first."

Ben shook his head before taking her from Jones's grasp. "Thank you for catching her."

"Anytime." He nodded. "I didn't think she'd actually try to hit me though?" He arched his brow at him before giving Holly the once-over.

"Me either."

Just then, Holly could hear little footsteps running their way. "You tried to hit a police officer?" Jimmy asked, once he was next to them.

Oh crap.

"Ummm." Holly was at a loss for words. She was blaming her reaction on the pregnancy hormones. Normally she would never have threatened anyone, no less actually move to take a swing.

"No," Officer Jones stepped in. "She was playing around."

Did he really just save her? *Thank you, Officer Jones! Maybe he isn't so bad. Huh? You know what I don't even know his first name. Maybe I should ask him—*

"Oh, like how we pranked her?"

Holly watched as Ben's eyes widened at Jimmy's declaration. *Prank?* Holly's eye's narrowed on the Officer, she took it back, she didn't care what his name was. Better yet, she was going to murder her husband. She turned back to Jimmy. "What did you say?"

"Way to let the cat out of the bag, squirt."

"This was your idea?" Holly sent Ben an evil glare.

"It was a bonding experience." Ben shrugged before winking at her.

Oh, I'm going to kill him. Didn't he understand he almost gave her a heart attack? "And you thought it was a good idea to recruit this big lug to help you?" Holly jerked her thumb over her shoulder to point at Officer Jones.

"Excuse me?"

"Lay off it, Mr. Scary Police Officer, dude." Holly snapped her attention to Jones. "You'll get your wish and be able to arrest me seeing as your about to be a witness to murder."

At that, Ben burst into uncontrollable laughter as he pulled Holly into his arms giving her a smacking kiss on the lips. "Love you, Grace. You make each day better than the last."

"Hate you."

Ben kissed her lips again. "No, you love me."

"Sometimes."

"All the time."

"You're not supposed to hit people or murder them," Jimmy announced, bringing their attention to him.

"That's right, squirt." Holly moved out of Ben's arms to talk to Jimmy. "I don't know what came over me. You never raise your hands to anyone, especially not a police officer. They are here to help us. We respect them." Holly wanted to pat herself on the back. This was her first 'mom' moment. She looked past the fact she almost tried to punch out a police officer and decided she was doing a good job.

"I think you should go in timeout."

Holly's mouth almost hit the ground.

"I agree," Officer Jones said which caused Holly to dart a glare in his direction.

"No more peanut butter glazed donuts for you," Jimmy announced proud of his punishment decision.

"What?" she cried. "You can't do that."

"I think Jimmy just did." Ben tried but failed to hold back his laugh.

"Why is it everyone is against me?" she cried as the image of her donuts melted away from her.

"You're fun entertainment." Ben pulled her into his arms as he continued to laugh at the situation.

"Jimmy," Henry called from the porch, who'd been watching the whole show. "Come help me eat the rest of the donuts." Henry smirked.

"Okay!" Jimmy ran back to Henry with his sights set on her treats.

"I'm gonna murder you," Holly growled narrowing her eyes at Ben.

"Not while Officer Jones is here." Ben looked at Jones. "Thanks."

"Anytime, now go enjoy your family." Jones whistled as he walked back to his police car.

"I really am going to kill you," Holly mumbled.

"No, you won't," Ben replied. "I have two donuts hidden for you."

As Holly looked into Ben's eyes and saw his playfulness and love, her heart melted. Sure, she was still going to kill him for siccing Officer Jones on her in the first place, but anyone willing to hide her donuts deserved all the love. "I love you, Ben."

"I know you do." Ben whistled for Waffles and Ripley, who had been pacing in the back of the car during the whole ordeal to follow them into the house. "Let's get your momma those well-deserved donuts. Just don't tell Jimmy."

"Why not?"

"I need to stay his favorite parent."

"Sorry to inform you of this, but that title goes to Waffles." Holly laughed along with Ben. "Now bring my car into the driveway." She shoved her keys at him. "If you're a good boy I'll reward you later."

Ben placed his hand on her stomach as he brought his lips to hers. "I'm counting on it."

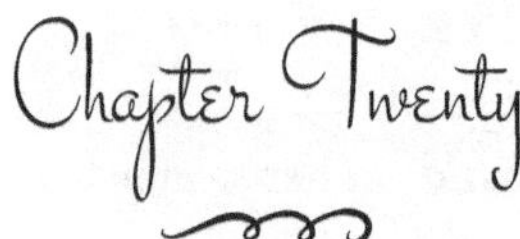

Chapter Twenty

HOLLY DRAGGED herself into the library. It had definitely been an eventful few weeks, to say the least. Holly wanted to believe she was immune and everything would be perfect, and most of the time it was. She wouldn't deny that. She loved her new life, but... she'd be a liar liar pants on fire if she didn't say it wasn't hard.

Plus, her sleep had been damn near non-existent since Jimmy moved in a few weeks ago. Add that to the fact Peanut now considered her insides a punching bag and it was a recipe for no sleep and a grumpy mood.

Holly pulled herself to the desk before plopping down. Her hand went to her stomach as it did most of the time.

This morning had been particularly rough. And she was still feeling the aftermath.

Ben had woken early to make Jimmy waffles.

Yes, waffles...one of her favorite foods. Before becoming a host to the creature overtaking her body, the sweet smell of the deliciously fluffy goodness would've had her mouth watering like it was Niagara Falls.

Not anymore.

On the contrary, the moment the delicious waffle smell hit her nose, it was like a violent punch to her stomach. Holly ended up running to the bathroom so fast it made her own head spin.

And that was exactly where she stayed.

The. Whole. Morning.

Jimmy and Ben ate their breakfast in peace while Holly tried having a heart-to-heart with Peanut. It did no good, though. Try as she might to get Peanut to understand waffles were her friends not the enemy, anytime she opened the bathroom door and got a whiff she was back hunched over the toilet.

See, rough morning.

Waffles, my fluffy delicious waffles, why do you have to be so traitorous? Holly sighed as she started rubbing her belly.

"Oh, oh!" Mildred appeared out of nowhere and ran right toward Holly with her eyes focused on her stomach. "Is Peanut kicking?" Once she was in front of Holly, she pushed Holly's hands off her stomach before replacing them with her own.

"No." Holly rolled her eyes. "You do realize this is creepy, right?"

Mildred started moving her hands around Holly's belly searching. "It's only creepy if you make it creepy."

Holly cocked her brow as she pushed Mildred's hands away. "*You're* making it creepy."

"You're grumpy again."

"And you're annoying."

"You do know, each time you say that all I hear is, 'Mildred, you're the most amazing person in the world never change, right?" Mildred's eyes brightened as she looked at Holly. "Never stop telling me."

Ignoring her, Holly groaned as she sat further into her chair closing her eyes. *Universe, I know you think this is funny, but with the morning I've had strangling this old bat and receiving nothing but bad karma is looking more and more worth it.*

"Are you gonna tell me?"

Holly opened her eyes to see Mildred now perched on the side of the desk giving her a once-over. "Tell you what?"

"The amount of times we have this conversation is unsettling." Mildred shook her head. "It's a back and forth we don't need to have. I ask you what's wrong, you get all huffy and pretend it's nothing, then I threaten you and you give in. It's very tiring."

"You're telling me."

Mildred ignored Holly as she pulled out her pen and pad. "Spill."

"Just so you have shit to tell your *knitting* buddies? I don't think so."

Mildred tapped her pen on her chin. "I do need more gossip. It is after all my week to bring the juicy stuff." She wiggled her brows at Holly. "But I've already got all I need from an incident I was lucky enough to witness with that hottie fireman and his lady friend in a compromising position over in the romance section, on Tuesday." She scratched her chin. "I think he said his name was Hank, but I could be wrong. Anyway, see you're safe. This is you and me. What's got your twat in a knot?"

The things that came out of Mildred's mouth didn't surprise Holly anymore. That was a new one, though. Holly shook her head with a deep sigh. "I don't know. I think I might be overwhelmed."

"As you should be."

"Gee, thanks."

"Missy, what have I told you about that tone with me? *And* might I add that whole respect your elder's thing?"

Holly sent her a toothy grin. "Not to do it."

"Exactly!" Mildred winked her way before adding, "Respecting me is only a hassle."

Holly burst into a laughter. "Don't I know it."

Mildred put her pen and pad back into her apron before pointing at Holly's belly. "You're huge, your—"

"Wow," Holly interrupted.

"Don't sass me. You know I'm talking about the fact you look like you're about to pop."

Holly glared at her. "It's not my fault this little one in here only wants donuts. It's been seven and a half months of this." Holly crossed her arms over her chest in a huff. "It's just donuts though, Peanut won't let me eat waffles."

"Your dog?"

"No," Holly cried. "The food. The delicious, fluffy goodness."

"Waffles are overrated."

Holly held her hand over her heart. "Blasphemy."

"And might I remind you, on top of being seven and a half months pregnant you just started parenting a seven-year-old boy. Of course, you're overwhelmed."

"I don't know how people do it," Holly replied. "Jimmy is great, he really is. He's sweet, he helps us all the time, but then he gets these moments where he shuts down and I don't know what to do."

"That's understandable."

"But I want to fix it." Holly thought back to the night before when Jimmy came in from the backyard upset. She ran around the house trying everything she could to cheer him up, but nothing worked.

Not even Lord Waffles.

"You can't," Mildred stated as a matter-of-fact. "Jimmy has a lot going on in his mind. The best thing you and Benny boy can do is give him a safe place where he can feel his emotions."

Holly let out a deep breath. "I know you're right."

"But, you don't. Jimmy lost both his parents in a horrific way. It doesn't matter how much time has passed from that, he's still going to have to come to terms with it."

"It hurts my heart when he shuts down."

"That's called love, dear." Mildred softened as she looked at Holly. "Have you talked to Ben about this?"

"No." Holly closed her eyes. "I don't want him to know I'm freaking out."

"That's silly. Talk to him."

"I can't. I don't want him to think I can't handle this."

Mildred shook her head as she tsked at her. "I never pegged you for an idiot."

"Hey, I'm not an idiot. I take offense to that."

"Don't you think Ben is having the same feelings you are?"

"Ben's not pregnant."

Mildred rolled her eyes. "Okay, fine, he probably isn't having the exact same feelings as you, but they're probably pretty close. Remember the key to a good marriage is communication and right now you both have to work on that. You've taken a child into your home all the while preparing to bring another one in."

Damn, score one for Mildred.

Holly sat back as Mildred's words sunk in. "When did you get so wise?"

"Today I have my Psychologist Mildred hat on." She shrugged.

Holly laughed with a shake of her head. "Have you been reading the self-help books and case studies again?"

Mildred winked. "You can't leave me to my own devices."

"I know."

"Next week I'm thinking of picking up woodworking books."

"Why?"

"Your baby shower is in a few weeks. I need to have something for you."

"Why don't you knit me something in your *knitting group*?"

"That would be boring. Nah, I think I'm gonna whittle you something." Mildred hopped off the desk and started heading toward the craft section of the library.

"Don't hurt yourself!"

Mildred turned back giving her the eye. "For that missy, I'm going to whittle you a cock."

Holly's eyes widened. "What?"

"A Cockatoo. What did you think I meant?" She winked.

"With you? I never know."

Mildred laughed as she turned back in search of whittling books.

Holly closed her eyes as she felt the start of a headache. Mildred was making her a tiny dick out of wood.

She knew it.

"WHAT'S WRONG?" Ben froze the moment he stepped into the bedroom that evening and looked at Holly. She sat on the edge of their bed with her hand over her stomach with tears in her eyes. "Babe?" He rushed to her side dropping to his knees in front of her.

Holly worried her bottom lip refusing to look at him.

Fuck. He scolded himself. The moment Holly excused

herself for the night he *knew* he should have gone after her. The past few weeks had been a lot. Ben had never taken the time to sit down and talk with Holly. And, now he was kicking himself.

The moment she arrived home from work he saw she was at her breaking point. "Holly please talk to me."

When she finally looked at him, it was like a sucker punch to the gut. She had a fear in her eyes, that broke him. "Baby…"

"I'm sorry," she whispered.

He cupped her face in his hands. "Why are you sorry? Talk to me."

Holly averted her eyes away from him, but he held her chin forcing her to look his way. "Grace?"

A tear fell down Holly's cheek. "I feel like I'm doing everything wrong, Ben. Jimmy's fine and then he's not. Then I get more heartburn and I think I've done something to hurt the baby. I haven't written a word in months. I should be able to handle everything that comes my way. As Dad likes to say, we're Flanagan's. Flanagan's can handle anything. I mean technically I'm a Richman now, but it's all the same. You're really strong, so I should be really strong, too. And I'm scared to death that telling you this you'll be disappointed in me. You'll think I'm not cut out for all of this even though we thought we were. I love that we have Jimmy here. I love that we have this little one." She placed her hand on her stomach. "But right now, I feel like I'm drowning and no matter how hard I try I can't keep my head above water."

Ben pulled her into his arms holding her tightly. His heart fucking broke at her words. How in the hell hadn't he seen this before? He was pissed at himself. With focusing on Jimmy getting settled, he neglected to see Holly struggling.

He felt like shit. But more importantly, he now knew he wasn't alone. He pulled back looking Holly in the eyes, trying to convey everything he felt. "Holly, baby, I would never be disappointed in you."

"I'm failing."

"You're not." He kissed her lips. "Can I tell you a secret?" He kissed her again. "I feel the same way. One second I'm ecstatic we have Jimmy and this little one coming. The next, I feel like I'm running on empty and I'm terrified, Holly. I can't shake the feeling I'm going to be a horrible dad."

"What?" Holly asked in shock. "You'd never be a horrible dad. It's not in your blood, Ben."

"You know how my mother was. I worry every day I'll end up like her. I can't help having those thoughts."

"Ben," Holly cried, tears spilling from her eyes. "Don't ever think that. You are nothing like her."

"But I can't help it, much like you can't help how you feel. Every decision I make I second-guess if I'm making the right choice. For Jimmy, for you, for Peanut. Every time I see Jimmy shut down I wonder if I could've done better. Or, if there is something else I could do." He kissed her forehead. "We took on a lot. I've never been happier in my life. There is absolutely no disputing that, but going from just us and the pets, to having a seven-year-old and you being pregnant is an adjustment."

"I wanted everything to be perfect."

"It is," Ben answered, looking deep into her eyes. "Because we have each other."

The room fell into silence for a few minutes until Holly spoke. "I didn't know you were feeling the same way."

Ben looked at Holly and saw the love pouring out of her eyes. "I'm sorry I didn't bring it up. We were bound to get a little overwhelmed." He gave her a half-smile. "Next time we ever get this way we talk about it, okay?"

"I love you, Ben."

"I love you, too."

"Do you think Jimmy is happy here?" Holly worried her bottom lip.

"I'd like to think so." Ben placed his hands on her belly. "And I'd like to think once this little one gets here they'll be happy too."

"I worry a lot."

"I know you do."

"I want to be a good mom. I want to be there for Jimmy. And, I want to be there for you." Holly looked at him, tears forming in her eyes again.

"You're always here for me. Jimmy loves you and I love you. So does Peanut." Ben grabbed the hem of her shirt lifting it over her head. Ben kept his focus on her eyes as he unclasped her bra tossing it behind him.

"What are you doing?"

Ignoring her, Ben grabbed the waistband of her pants pulling them so she was forced to lift her hips. Once she was fully undressed, he stood doing the same.

"Ben?" She cocked her head to the side.

"Shh." Ben scooped her into his arms, bringing her to her side of the bed. He then gently tucked her into the sheets before getting into bed himself. Once he was positioned, he pulled her close to him wrapping his arms around her.

They needed this.

They needed the time in each other's arms.

As silly as that might seem, he knew. He kissed her forehead. "Promise me, whenever you feel like you're drowning, you'll talk to me. I'll be your life vest." He kissed her wedding ring. "You're mine. And *I* promise whenever I feel like I can't handle this, I'll do the same."

"I promise."

"This is you and me against the world, babe. Not us separately against the world."

Holly nodded.

Ben pulled her closer to him feeling her skin against his as he held her in his arms. "I love you, Grace."

"I love you too, Ben."

After a few minutes, Holly fell soundly asleep in his arms. And for the first time in weeks Ben felt that no matter what happened or what would happen, as long as the both of them were on the same page, they could get through anything.

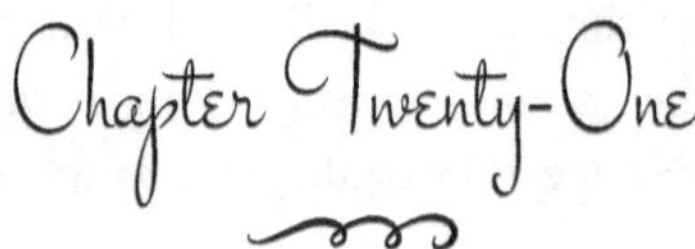

Chapter Twenty-One

AFTER BEN and Holly's heart-to-heart a few weeks ago, everything seemed to fall right into place. They both had made it a point to have a conversation every night before bed. Jimmy had settled in considerably well, and their love for him only grew more and more as the days went on. And thankfully, Jimmy loved Henry. Once every other week Henry and Jimmy had a sleepover that also included the dogs.

It gave Holly and Ben a guaranteed date night. Which in turn only made them stronger.

And Ben was downright grateful for that.

But right now, Ben wanted to be as far away from their house as humanly possible.

Who in the hell knew all the work that went into planning a baby shower? For freaking real.

As Holly, Emma, and Mildred added the finishing touches to the party, Ben had stolen Jimmy and got the hell out of there.

No offense to all the ladies going above and beyond to make it perfect for him and Holly but damn. First, you had Mildred trying to sneak in dick lollipops onto the dessert table. Emma was putting up streamers and then saying they looked like shit and ripping them down only to put them back up again *in the same spot.*

Waffles was causing havoc trying to steal the presents.

Seriously, he took one of the gifts that was on the floor and carried it to Jimmy's room and ripped it open. Ripley and Twitch were running around like it was endless play time.

Then there was Holly.

Ben lost count of the number of times she'd run into the wall, countertop, tripped over the rug, banged her knee against the coffee table, you name it, she did it. At this point, he didn't think his heart could take a second more. If he watched Holly nearly impale herself on a spatula one more time, he'd lose it.

"Are we going to get Grandpa Henry?" Jimmy asked, from the passenger seat of the SUV.

"Yep, and John."

Jimmy looked at him with a wide smile that brightened his eyes. "I like Mr. John. He does weird things."

That's an understatement.

"And he always seems to be in a fight with Lord Waffles," Jimmy giggled.

"That's 'cause John's a child most of the time."

"Like me?"

"No," Ben answered. "I'd say you're more mature than he is."

"It's fun to watch when he gets into fights with Waffles."

Ben winked at him. "You only think that 'cause Waffles normally wins."

"True."

"Are you excited for the party today, squirt?"

"I guess so." Jimmy looked out the window.

Ben watched him from the corner of his eye trying to think of something to say. "You like Mildred, I'm sure she will make you laugh."

"She does." He kept his gaze out of the window.

"You okay, squirt?"

"I'm okay."

Jimmy wasn't okay, but Ben didn't know what else to say. Maybe he could lighten the mood. "How about after we get Grandpa Henry and John we stop by the donut shop?"

Apparently, that's exactly what Ben needed to say.

Jimmy's face shot toward his with a massive smile on his face. "Can I get the cream-filled one?"

"Sure."

"I used to never get donuts at my other houses. But with you and Holly I get them all the time."

Ben grimaced. *Great, let's start him young on unhealthy habits.* "Don't tell Carol that."

"I'll think about it." A mischievous grin appeared on Jimmy's face.

"Why you little..." Ben tried not to laugh as he placed his hand over his heart in shock. "Are you playing me? Was your end game a donut all this time?"

"Maybe."

Ben shook his head impressed as a slow smile spread across his face. If he wasn't positive before, he was now. Jimmy fit in perfectly with them. "Where did you learn to get this good?"

"Waffles."

"Figures."

It only took around thirty minutes to get Henry and John, along with gathering the donuts as a surprise for Holly.

However, Ben should have known nothing was ever as simple as it would have been for anyone else.

Nope. Not even in the slightest.

Ben lost track of the number of times he had to threaten John to stop going into the donut box. It was like he had *two* seven-year-olds in the car.

John actually had the gall to look into the rearview mirror

at Ben after he'd sworn he hadn't touched any, with copious amounts of powdered sugar on his face.

Like he said. Two seven-year-olds.

Throw in Henry trying to bribe Jimmy in sending up some donuts his way too. Foolish Ben for thinking having John sit in the back seat with Jimmy would have been fine.

From now on the donuts go in the trunk of the car.

Thankfully, they were pulling onto his street. He just prayed there was at least one donut left for Holly.

As he pulled into the driveway, Ben was reminded why he left in the first place. Mildred had run out onto the porch with a diaper on her head that had a drawing of a crown on it.

What in the absolute fuck was he about to walk into?

UNIVERSE, save me now!

Holly looked around the living room and did her best not to freak the fuck out. She should have known better than to leave the planning to Mildred. Thank God, Holly had gotten Emma to agree to help.

Sure, Emma was a little frightened after meeting Mildred the first time—wasn't everyone? But nonetheless, she agreed to help rein Mildred in.

Foolishly Holly thought having Emma as co-planner would have given her a simple quiet gathering as they celebrated baby Peanut.

But no.

Not one freaking bit.

And Holly knew better. Take for instance, right now John and Ben were in a battle to the death. Sure, she knew they were competitive, like hardcore competitive, but this, this was over the top. She had never heard so much trash-talk in her life.

Holly had to apologize to Martha, Will's wife, and then send Jimmy out back to shield his young ears.

Want to know the kicker? All this hustle and bustle was for the title of *King of the Baby Shower* which included their own diaper hat with a crown drawn on it.

That's right. All the winner got was a freaking diaper crown.

Sure, it was decked out pretty nicely, Holly had to admit and all but it was still a diaper.

Holly watched as Ben and John duked it out in the new game. The one where if you got another person at the party to say the word, *baby,* you got a stupid little clothespin. The one at the end with the most clothespins won the crown.

By the looks of it, Ben seemed to be in the lead, but not by much. And if the look John was sending Ben was any indication of how things were going, Holly was ninety percent sure there was about to be a full-on brawl between the two.

Lord help her when they start the 'guess the baby food' game. She knew there was a food fight in her future.

Looking past the insaneness that was her husband and John, Mildred's husband kept sneaking to the dessert table and munching down the goodies. Right now, the table was nearly empty. The only reason she knew was because she usually met him at the table sneaking in her own treats.

At this point, the party was about to run out of desserts, her husband and John were minutes from a fistfight, Waffles thought everything in the room was his and that was that, and finally there was a crazy old bat wearing a diaper on her head.

Welcome to my life.

"Come on, Emma, don't be a poor sport, play along. What's Holly got in her belly?" John begged Emma as he cornered her in the room, his evil glare at Ben forgotten.

Holly watched as Emma looked right at her, shook her

head with a smile on her face and looked back at John. "About half a donut."

Which was true since Holly still had the other half in her hand. Holly laughed. *One point, Emma. Zero points, John.*

With a growl and then a pout John shot his attention to Holly. She then lifted her donut in the air before taking another bite.

"That's not fair."

"All is fair in a competition." Emma smirked.

"You're not even playing."

"I'm playing. My goal is to make it so you don't get my clothespin but Ben does." Emma fingered the tiny clothespin on the collar of her shirt.

"Really?" John's eyes narrowed as another growl escaped him. "I'm filing this away to bring up later. And make no mistake, Emma, I *will* be bringing it back up." He leaned in closer. Holly couldn't make out what he whispered in Emma's ear but with her face going completely red, she had an idea.

Just to make sure though, Holly pulled out her phone sending herself a text message to remind her to interrogate Emma.

Inquiring minds want to know after all.

Emma stepped back before clearing her throat. "You talk an awful lot of game for a dentist."

"Do you want to know what's the best part of me being a dentist?" He stared at her lips. "I'm damn well educated in all things dealing with the human mouth... especially the *tongue*."

Emma swallowed.

Time to step in... Holly started making her way over to them.

"I'm up to five!" Ben hollered from the other side of the room as he placed another clothespin on his sleeve.

"Shit!" John jumped back from Emma scanning the room. When he saw Mildred's husband still had his clothespin, he set his sights on him. Before leaving, however, he turned back to Emma. "This isn't over."

Oh, the lunch date this week was going to be an interesting one. Holly added more notes to the back of her mind to bring up as she stopped next to Emma.

"Ignore him," Emma said, looking at her.

"Not on your life, but I will wait until our weekly lunch date to bring it up."

Emma paled before searching the room trying to avoid Holly's eyes.

"Uhh, this has been fun." Emma bit her bottom lip desperately trying to change the subject.

"Sure, let's go with fun," Holly replied.

"If you think this is a good time you should have seen what I originally had planned," Mildred said, coming up to them still wearing that ridiculous diaper on her head.

"I'm pretty sure what you had planned was considered a bachelorette party, *not* a baby shower." Emma's eyes twinkled as she smirked at Mildred.

"If done right, one causes the other doesn't it?" Mildred looked Emma up and down.

Do I now need to worry about a fistfight between these two?

"In your eyes, Mildred," Emma answered, with a shake of her head.

"Hey, it's not my fault you all don't know entertainment when you see it. I was all set to have some hunky men in uniform show up and try to arrest us." Mildred got this dreamy look in her eyes, before she turned to glare at Emma. "But this one went behind my back and canceled it."

Emma took a small step behind Holly shielding herself. "She scares me."

"Me too." Holly smiled before turning back to the old coot. "I would have canceled it too. A baby shower does not need a striptease." Holly turned to Emma. "Thank you for looking out for me."

"Anytime. Speaking of looking out." Emma nodded her head toward John. "Let me go help him. I think Will's about five seconds from arresting him."

Holly turned her head to see John bouncing on his feet begging for Will to answer his question. "You're right. Will does look like he's about had it."

"Wait a second," Mildred jumped in, cocking her brow at Emma. "I thought you hated him?"

"I never said that." Emma's eyes widened.

Mildred did that creepy silent thing as she gave Emma the once-over. Then a wicked smile appeared on her face. "No, dear. Indeed, you didn't."

Then in a flash, Mildred was gone.

"What the hell just happened?" Emma asked as Holly stood there in shock.

"I'm not sure but I think Mildred just looked into your soul and found out all your secrets."

"It did seem that way didn't it?"

"As it normally does with her."

"Pumpkin," Henry yelled, getting Holly's attention. "Come on it's gift time. Stop running your chompers and get your butt over here."

Holly rolled her eyes. *Parents...* She placed her hand on her stomach. *Don't ever let me say shit like that, okay, Peanut?* She looked back at her father with a shake of her head. "We told everyone not to bring anything. We didn't need it."

"And yet we still did!" Mildred squawked from the couch.

"Yeah, you don't show up to a baby shower empty-handed. That's not how this works," Martha agreed, as Will placed his arm around his wife.

"Fine. Have it your way." Holly shook her head as she made her way to the seat that was placed in the front of the room. Ben quickly plopped down next to her. "Do you see how many clothespins I have?" he asked, showing off his arm like it was a trophy.

"Yes, babe. You did such a good job." Holly gave his knee a pat.

Ben puffed out his chest. "I've got two more than John."

"Hey, this game isn't over until the old lady says it is." John glared at him.

"Who you callin' old, buddy?" Mildred stared John down. "For that you lose a point."

"Hey now, that wasn't in the rules."

"I make the rules. You've only lost one, you want to make it two?"

John mumbled something as he threw himself into the nearby chair in a huff.

Mildred turned back to Emma giving her the *look*. "I didn't say anything." Emma held up her hands.

"Just checking."

Out of the corner of Holly's eyes she saw Ben puff out again. *Oh, for the love of all things.*

"Here you go, Holly." Jimmy held out the gift Waffles had ripped apart earlier to her.

My heart. "Thank you, squirt."

Jimmy sat at her feet as she opened the present. It was a light green crocheted baby blanket from Emma. "Thank you, sweetie."

Emma's face reddened. "You're welcome. I made it myself."

"You did?"

Emma placed a stray piece of her hair behind her ear. "Yeah. I kinda picked up crocheting a while back."

"It's beautiful." Holly squeezed it. She felt tears coming to her eyes. *Damnit! These damn pregnancy hormones. They will be the death of me.*

"Thank you, Emma. That's really sweet." Ben smiled at her.

"Can you make me a blanket?' John asked.

"I'll make you a muzzle."

"If it comes from you, I don't care *what* it is." John's whole face brightened.

"Knock it off you two." Mildred glared at them. "Keep going."

In order to avoid the wrath of Mildred, that's exactly what they did. Slowly, her and Ben opened their gifts one by one thanking everyone as they went.

That's when Holly came to the last box. Not thinking much of it, she ripped it open, pulling the top off. The second her eyes focused on what was inside she snapped the lid back on.

Oh, no. Please no.

Holly carefully peeked inside. *Holy shit. I'll kill her.*

Holly held the box with a death grip.

"What is it?" Ben asked, trying to take the box from her.

"Yeah, Holly." Mildred winked at her. "What's in the box?"

Holly narrowed her eyes at the crazy old woman before turning to Ben shaking her head. *Please drop the subject.*

Ben cocked his brow at her before easily prying the box from her grip. When he opened it, he erupted in a deep belly laugh that filled the whole room.

Holly snapped her attention to Mildred as everyone started asking what was going on.

Inside the box was indeed a tiny wooden cock. And, no it was definitely not a bird.

Holly glared at Mildred, and all that crazy old woman did was wink at her.

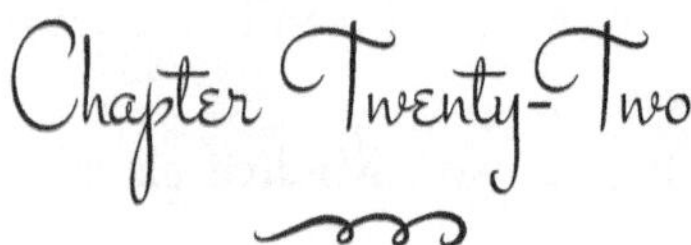

Chapter Twenty-Two

HOLLY PLACED her hand on her stomach as another pain raced through her. She was getting really tired of it. She knew it was nothing more than stress, but over the last three days the pain had gotten worse. At this point, she was ready to murder someone.

She was ungodly huge. Being able to see her toes: nope. Hadn't seen them in months.

Bending over to pick up after Jimmy was done playing: negatory. Bending was *not* an option.

Holly looked around the living room at dog toys *and* human toys thrown all around.

Maybe this was just going to be her life from now on.

It could be worse.

A crippling pain shot through her lower back. "Eff me," she growled. Holly looked to the ceiling. *Remind me to kill Ben when he gets home. If this is what it's like being pregnant, he's never coming anywhere near me with his dick again.*

She tried standing up as straight as she could. *Kill me now!*

"Holly, do you need some help?" Jimmy asked, running

into the living room. He quickly picked up the dog toy Holly was trying to grab and handed it to her.

"Thanks, squirt." She ruffled his hair.

Waffles started running around the living room trying to get Jimmy to chase him. "Hold on, Waffles, we gotta make sure Holly doesn't need anything else." Jimmy looked at her expectantly completely ready to do whatever she needed.

Her heart melted.

Jimmy was terrific in so many ways. He was always by her side helping her with anything she needed. If he saw her struggling with anything and Ben wasn't around, he was there in an instant. When she tripped over an invisible rock, Jimmy always seemed to grab her hand or arm to steady her.

He was a little Ben.

And then there was his nighttime ritual. Holly and Ben would tuck him in, making sure Ripley and Twitch were nestled with him. Jimmy without fail, would hug Holly resting his head on her stomach, giving it a squeeze telling Peanut he'd be there in the morning and he was only a few rooms away.

Even though Holly knew it was coming, she still ended up a blubbering mess by the time she got to her bedroom.

Jimmy fit perfectly into their family.

Holly smiled warmly, even with all the pain she was in.

Life was good.

Then Waffles started barking.

Holly rolled her eyes. *Well, it's as good as it's gonna get.* Waffles ran full speed at Jimmy trying to get him to play.

Waffles...

As if he knew, Waffles turned his attention to Holly. He barked once, then trotted toward the back door offended.

Holly rolled her eyes even harder this time. God forbid anyone threw a wrench in anything Waffles wanted.

Waffles looked at Holly over his shoulder.

Sorry me being pregnant is an inconvenience to you.

Waffles huffed agreeing with her.

Holly narrowed her eyes at her dog. *I'll remember this.*

"When's Ben coming home?" Jimmy asked, distracting her from the argument she was having with Waffles.

Jimmy looked down to see Twitch rubbing against his legs so he plucked him into his arms.

"Soon, I hope." Holly looked past Jimmy to glare at Waffles some more.

Jimmy looked at Twitch as he scratched under his chin. "Uh, do you think when he gets home we can go to the dog park? I kinda promised Waffles and Ripley we'd go today."

That's where the attitude from Waffles was coming from. She glared at her dog who was now plopped onto his butt staring her down.

"Oh, you did now?" she asked still in the stare down with Lord Waffles.

"They are kinda hard to say no to when they give you that look." Holly broke her standoff with her dog to see Jimmy biting his bottom lip. When she looked back at Waffles, he was now giving *her* the look. *Why you little shit!* "Are you trying to manipulate my boy?"

Waffles huffed.

He was. Oh, let me at him! Waffles turned his nose up, defying her. "Young man, you do not manipulate your brother. Jimmy doesn't have to do anything you say." Holly crossed her arms over her chest. *Take that, Waffles.*

Oh, he took it all right. He sent Holly an evil look before walking over to Jimmy. The bastard then fell over onto his back demanding scratches.

Jimmy was instantly on his knees giving in to the little devil's demands. To make matters worse, out of the corner of his eye, Waffles had the audacity to look at her as if saying *he* was the one in charge here.

"I'm telling your father." Waffles barked at her. "Don't back sass me."

Waffles flipped over onto his front with a huff before staring her down again. This caused Jimmy to burst into laughter.

"Don't encourage him."

Jimmy looked at her with the exact same look Waffles got in his eyes when he was causing havoc. "I'll think about it."

Oh my God, there is two of them now. Wait, three when you add in Ripley. Holly plucked Twitch into her arms, who'd been sitting on the floor after Jimmy let him go. *At least I have you.*

Twitch then jumped out of her arms and ran over to Ripley who was on the couch watching the show.

Wonderful. Holly shook her head. "You hang around Waffles too much."

"That's 'cause I love him." Jimmy smiled brightly at her.

She leaned down and kissed the top of his head. "He loves you too. Why don't you go outside and play for a little while until Ben gets home?"

"Okay!" You didn't have to tell Jimmy twice. He took off running toward the back door with Waffles and Ripley by his side.

Poor Twitch. He sat at the back door. He then looked back at her. "Oh, now I'm good enough for you?"

Twitch's head flicked as he stared at her. "Fine. Come here little one." Twitch ran to Holly. "They'll be back in soon then you can go back to pretending I don't exist while they're in the house." Twitch started purring in her arms.

Figures.

"I've got them, Grace!" Ben rushed through the front door nearly scaring Holly to death. She placed her hand over her heart. *I think I just peed.*

Then Ben's words registered. "Wait, what did you say?" She stared at him with bated breath.

"I've got them." Ben held up the papers in his hand.

"Are you kidding? Don't play with me Benjamin, it won't end well for you."

Ben pulled her close before giving her a kiss. "Not even a little bit, Grace. Here are the approved adoption papers for Jimmy."

Holly screamed in excitement. "Is this really happening?"

"You bet your sweet ass it is!" Ben brought his lips to hers once more kissing the ever-loving daylights out of her.

They had worked so hard to get to this point. They'd had countless appointments with their lawyers, supervised visits with the social worker, you name it, and it all came down to this moment.

This was what they had been waiting for.

Jimmy was going to officially be theirs.

Forever.

"What are we waiting for? Let's go tell him." The moment Holly took a step toward the back door she froze causing Ben to stare at her with his brows pulled together. "What's wrong, babe?" He cocked his head to the side.

That's not pee.

"Uhh, Ben, I think my water just broke."

Chapter Twenty-Three

HOLY FUCK!

Ben stared at Holly who was completely frozen with her legs spread slightly apart. He gave her the quick once-over, but his mind wouldn't catch up. There was no way in hell he heard her right. Holly wasn't due for another two weeks.

Two weeks.

Yet, Holly stood there her eyes wide, her mouth partly open, and her face pale.

Maybe it was a cramp? Yeah, that's what it was. Ben looked her up and down again. *No, this was it.* His heart slammed against his chest.

The doctor said two weeks. That meant they had two weeks. That was fourteen days.

Doctors can't do the whole *oops* thing. There were no takesie backsies in this situation.

"Ben?"

He snapped his attention to Holly, who hadn't moved a muscle. "He said we had two weeks! Two. Weeks." Ben's eyes widened. "Doctors get paid to be right about this stuff. Where the hell is the accountability?"

"Are you always right?"

Ben puffed out his chest. "Are you questioning my medical knowledge?"

"No." She shook her head. "I'm saying sometimes things change and right now Peanut has decided they want out. Two weeks be damned."

Ben made a mental note to send the doctor a very strongly worded email about their timelines once the baby was here.

Holy fuck their child was about to be born!

"Are you just gonna stand there?" Holly asked, still not moving.

At her words, Ben finally snapped into action. *Holy fuck it was happening.* In an instant, Ben started running around the house like a madman.

He ran to their bedroom where Holly's hospital bag was packed. Thank fuck he'd made her do it last week.

He then ran into the bathroom. When he got there, he had absolutely no idea why he went in there to begin with.

Fuck it.

He knew he didn't have time to question anything. So instead, he threw open the medicine cabinet, and with an aggressive arm sweep, he tossed everything into her hospital bag.

Better to be safe than sorry. It didn't matter he'd also tossed into the bag his aftershave. Deciding not to care, he zipped up the bag, threw it over his shoulder and sprinted into the living room. That's when he saw Holly's new favorite blanket. The one Emma had made. Quickly he snatched it into his hands before throwing it around his neck.

Ben ran full speed out the front door. Once he got to his SUV, he tossed everything inside before taking off around the house to the backyard.

"Ben! You're home! Now we can go to the dog park." Jimmy's face lit up.

"Not this time, kiddo," Ben yelled as he ran full speed toward him. "It's go-time."

Unfortunately for Ben, Waffles thought anyone running in the backyard meant it was time to play. Instantly Waffles swerved in between Ben's legs causing him to lose his footing.

Before Ben knew it, he was on the grass in a complete daze at what happened.

Was this how Holly felt?

Ben looked at Waffles who was giving him the side-eye, like *he* was offended it wasn't really play time.

Can anything be easy in their life? Waffles barked at him before prancing his way toward Jimmy. Yes, prancing, like the diva he was.

Ben shook his head as he stood. Quickly he brushed himself off before he turned his attention back to Jimmy.

"We gotta go, kiddo."

Without thinking Ben threw Jimmy over his shoulder before running through the backyard, taking the steps up to the house two at a time. All while ushering Ripley and Waffles into the house.

Through all the chaos and barking, Ben managed to get inside before locking the backdoor.

With Jimmy still on his shoulder he ran through the living room and back out the front door. When he made it to the car, as gently as he could he tossed Jimmy in the back seat before buckling him.

Once he was secured Ben ran around to the driver's side door before hopping in. He turned on the car and peeled out the driveway in route to the hospital never once looking back.

"Uh, Ben?" Jimmy spoke from the back seat.

Ben's heart raced as he rounded the corner of their neighborhood. "Yeah?" Right now, his only focus was getting to the hospital.

"I think you forgot something."

Ben's brows pulled together. No, he hadn't forgotten anything. He'd planned this out in his head a hundred times. He had their hospital bag, Holly's blanket that Emma made, and then... "Oh, fuck!" Ben slammed on the brakes causing the car to come to a screeching halt.

Holy fucking shit. He hit his hand on the steering wheel. He'd seen this in movies tons of times, but he never thought it actually happened in real life.

He fucking forgot Holly.

With a U-turn that he was sure was illegal on how fast he peeled around the corner he raced back to the house.

HOLLY LOOKED DOWN AT WAFFLES. "Do you think he realized he forgot me?" she asked. Waffles barked before walking into the living room plopping down onto his stomach ignoring her.

"Love you too, Waffles."

Holly was a tad freaked out. Okay, she was way more than a tad freaked. She was about to push a human out of her va-jay-jay. A human. That's cause to be terrified. Regardless though, she found herself chuckling at seeing Jimmy thrown over Ben's shoulder as he ran through the house. Holly and Jimmy had even shared a "what's going on" look before Ben carried him out of the house.

"Why were you not in the car?" Ben yelled, slamming through the front door.

Holly crossed her arms over her chest as she arched her brow.

"Don't give me that look, Grace. You could have gotten into the car."

Both of her brows shot to the ceiling as her hands went to her hips.

"Unknot your twat, buster, *you're the* one that forgot me. I just stood here and watched the show."

"Unknot my twat?" His brow raised.

A smile spread on both of their faces as they both said at the exact same time, "Mildred."

That's when another contraction hit her. *At least I now know I'm not dying.*

Ben was by her side in an instant. "You could have come to the car."

"And miss the show? Not on your life. It's not very often I get to see the calm, cool, collected Ben lose his fuckin' shit." Holly looked him up and down. "Why are your knees dirty?"

"Waffles tripped me."

"Really?" Holly smirked. "I thought you were too smooth to let his holiness ever get the better of you?"

Ben glared at her. "I'm gonna let that slide, but only 'cause you're about to give birth to my child."

"*Our* child."

Ben ignored her comment, scooping her into his arms bridal style. "I can walk."

His eyes narrowed at her. "Then you could have walked to the car."

"Good point." Holly wrapped her arms around Ben's neck as he carried her. "Do you think it was dumb to have waited until the baby pops out to find out what we're having?"

"That's what's running through your head right now?" he asked.

"Don't get snippy with me."

Ben shook his head. "Let's just get to the hospital." Carefully Ben got Holly into the car. It didn't help Jimmy was in the backseat laughing so hard he was snorting and threatening that he was about to pee on himself.

Ben sent Jimmy a glare too.

Poor Ben.

"I'm gonna pee!" Jimmy snorted again.

"Don't go joking about peeing on yourself." Holly looked at Jimmy. "I thought I had."

"Eww."

Preach it.

Holly gritted her teeth as she felt another contraction. *Oh, my God, I'm about to have a baby.* "Emma!"

"What about her?" Ben asked as he pulled out of their driveway.

"I promised her I'd call as soon as I went into labor." Holly grabbed her phone dialing her number. Emma swore to Holly she'd be there when the baby was born. She'd be the level head in case anything went wrong... like you know forgetting Holly.

Holly's call went straight to voicemail so she tried again. Nothing.

Oh God, what if something happened to Emma. What if—

"Holly, what's wrong?" Ben grabbed her hand. "Are you having another contraction?"

"Emma's not answering her phone."

Ben squeezed her hand tighter. "Calm down, Grace, it's okay. Maybe she's got no service."

Holly's heart pounded against her chest.

"Can you do me a favor and call John and let him know we're on the way to the hospital?" Ben asked.

Holly nodded as the realization started to sink in again. She was about to push out a child... She wasn't ready. Nope, not at all. "On second thought, I think we can turn around and go home."

"Excuse me?"

"I think all I did was pee on myself. Yep. That's it." Holly started bouncing her head up and down. "That's exactly what happened."

"That was your water breaking."

"Nope. Pee."

"Holly..." Ben looked at her as another contraction hit. *Stop it, Peanut! We aren't ready!*

"Holly you're holding your stomach and wincing."

"It's gas."

"Holly."

"Fine. Jerk." She took a deep breath before looking at her phone again. It took John four rings to finally pick up. *"Hello?"* he panted into the phone.

"Why are you breathing so hard?" Holly asked as she bit her bottom lip. This wasn't a full-on contraction but it still felt like there was a monster inside of her and it was clawing its way out.

"Why are you calling?" he countered in typical John fashion.

"What's with all the attitude from everyone today?" Holly snapped.

"I'm right in the middle of something here, Holly. You better be havin' that baby or I promise you, you thought I was a pain in the ass before you haven't seen—"

"Of course, I'm pushing out a child. Why else would I be calling?" She narrowed her eyes. That's it, John was officially off their Christmas card list. And this year she had a good photo planned. It involved her, Ben, Jimmy, all their pets, and elf costumes. It was gonna be freaking epic.

"Oh shit! I thought you had two weeks."

"Well apparently doctors lie. Even though it's their job and all, they can say whatever the hell they want."

Holly heard rustling on the other end of the phone. *"Fuck. Okay, we'll be right there."*

"Who's we?"

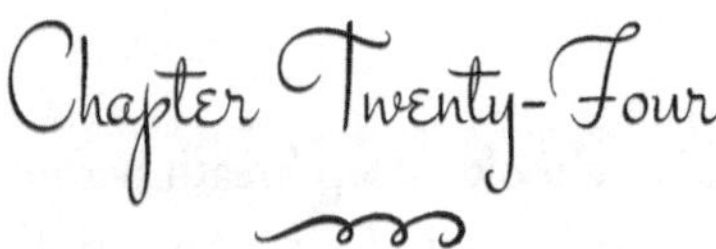

Chapter Twenty-Four

HOLLY WASN'T sure who was freaking out more, her or Ben. From the looks of it, she was leaning more toward Ben right now. At least she got happy drugs once she was admitted into the hospital.

Thank God.

Although, they weren't that happy since she was still in pain.

The moment Ben pulled into the hospital and hauled her out of the car, she was taken to the labor and delivery unit where they started an IV and told her she needed to wait. Unfortunately for her, she was too far along for the epidural, but not far enough to push.

She closed her eyes. *Universe, I thought we had this heart-to-heart already? Will you ever give me a fucking break?*

Holly clenched her hands as another contraction hit.

Nope. Read you loud and clear, Universe.

"How in the fuck do they think you're not ready?" Ben growled, looking at her. "You're wincing every few minutes."

"Language." Holly glared at him, before darting her eyes to Jimmy.

"That's okay, Ben said the same word when he realized he forgot you." Jimmy sent her a playful smile before looking at Ben.

"Oh, he did now?" Holly's eyes narrowed at her husband.

"Yep."

"I'm gonna remember this, kid." Ben snapped his attention to Jimmy, who shrugged.

Throw me a bone here universe and take me now. Holly threw her head back onto her pillow looking at the ceiling as she felt a sharp pain once again. *I mean Ben is right. Sure, I got meds to help but this kinda sucks. Okay, this really sucks. How in the hell do people pop out more than one kid?*

Ben grabbed her hand squeezing it. "Do you want me to force them to give you an epidural?"

"You can't force them to do anything." She gritted her teeth as the contraction went through her.

"I can try."

"It's fine. They said I was too far along. So, it wouldn't help anyway." With her luck, she'd get the thing, push out the kid, *then* end up going numb from the waist down.

"Do you want me to see if they can give you more pain meds? There has to be something they can do."

"No." Holly squeezed his hand. How had she gotten so lucky to have Ben? Even now he was trying to ease her pain any way he could. She looked at him as the contraction died down. There was so much concern in his eyes. "I just want this baby out."

"Two weeks my ass," Ben mumbled.

"Language!" Holly closed her eyes again. "But, you're not wrong."

"Is Peanut coming soon?" Jimmy asked, drawing Holly's attention to him.

"I hope so." *Even if I have to crawl up there myself and get Peanut out.*

Jimmy nodded before sinking back into the chair, looking down at his hands. Holly was about to say something when another pain started to creep in. Her heart raced as a new wave of panic washed over her.

This was it.

There was no going back now.

She was about to push a human out of her. A human she and Ben would be one hundred percent responsible for.

Holy crap on ten million crackers. I'm not ready!

As Holly was about to fall into a complete panic attack, John burst through the door. "Is it happening?"

"Does it look like Holly's pushing out a kid?" Ben scoffed.

"Hey, I don't know how these things work, for all I know she could have popped out the thing on the way to the hospital." John crossed his arms over his chest in defiance.

"Did you sleep through human anatomy in school?" Holly rolled her eyes at him. That's when she saw Emma emerge from behind John. To her surprise, John gave Emma a *knowing* look. "I know all about the human anatomy, so I didn't need to go."

"You were the *we?*" Holly asked, trying to make sense of what other dimension she was sure as hell she was in. Then John's words registered. "Oh my God!"

Emma jumped forward with her hands held up. "It's not what you're thinking."

"What am I thinking then?" Holly's voice raised.

Emma bit her lower lip as John straightened puffing out his chest. Holly moved her attention to Emma. *Oh missy, as soon as this kid comes out, you and I are having a conversation.* She looked John up and down as the pride radiated off him. *A long conversation.*

Emma must have read her mind since her eyes widened as her face lost its color.

That's right! Be prepared.

Just then another contraction hit Holly causing her to scream out in agony. This time it was by far the worst that she'd had. *Holy fuckity fuck. This one's bad. Why the hell was I so adamant that I was fine this morning? Why? Why am I like this? Maybe then I could have gotten the epidural.*

"Is the baby coming?" John asked.

"No. I'm singing the song of my fucking people."

"Language."

Holly snapped her head to Ben. When she saw his smirk, she didn't know whether she wanted to give him a point for calling her out or punch him in the throat.

Punch. Yeah, she was definitely going with punch.

Emma ran to Holly's side distracting her from the plot to kill her husband. "What do you need? Why aren't you pushing? What did we miss?"

Those were some damn good questions. Holly threw her head over to Ben. *Let him do the talking. It's his fault I'm here in the first place.*

"When we first got here, they said she was too far into labor for the epidural but not far enough to push," Ben answered. "They need to wait until her contractions are about two minutes apart."

"I'm not a doctor or anything but by the weird face thingy she is doing I'm gonna say she's two minutes apart," John announced.

"No shit." Holly snapped her attention to him. She then looked at Emma. "Remind me to poison him once I'm sprung free from this place."

"I won't eat your cooking again." John crossed his arms over his chest. "Been there, done that. Learned my lesson."

"Then I'll run you over with my car."

"You'll have to catch me first."

"Children..." Ben warned.

"Get used to it, Ben," Emma remarked, trying her hardest not to smile but was failing.

"You think I would be by now."

Holly squeezed Ben and Emma's hands as her contraction intensified. That's when she remembered. "My dad! We have to call my dad."

Jesus effing Christ. How in the hell had I forgotten to call my dad? I haven't even had the kid yet and I'm already failing.

"Taken care of," Ben said, drawing her attention to him. "I called once you were in the room. John had already left so I sent a taxi to get him."

Instantly some of Holly's unease left her as she observed Ben.

He stared down at her with so much love it was almost overwhelming. She needed to remember no matter what was happening she had him and they would get through everything together. He was her rock.

"I'm proud of you," he whispered using his other hand to cup her face, making sure to keep her attention on him. "Thank you for giving me this gift."

Just like that, everything was okay again. "I love you, Ben."

"I love you too, Grace."

"Uhh, Holly?"

Holly turned to Emma who was now biting her lip.

"Umm, Mildred's on her way too."

Holly brows shot to the ceiling. "She is?"

"Yeah, after John said you were in labor I kinda panicked and called her."

Holly threw her head back. Great, this was all she needed, Mildred yapping her jaw about how Holly wasn't pushing right or some crap like that. Holly could see it now. *"You gotta push that baby out like it's the only thing standin' between you and your man's dong again."* Holly recoiled. *Oh God, I'm even thinking like Mildred now.*

Before Holly could really let that thought sink in, the doctor, the one who had been on call when they came in walked into the room. "How are you feeling?"

"How does it look like I'm feeling?" Holly snapped.

"I did hear talk from the staff about this room." The doctor smiled brightly at them.

Can I add him to the list of people I can murder, Universe? I'll make it quick, you won't even know what happened.

"We think Holly's contractions have progressed," Ben said chiming in.

"Let's take a look here, shall we?"

Just then a frantic Mildred and Henry ran into the room. "Is my grandbaby here yet?" Henry asked.

"Where's the baby?" Mildred echoed.

"Fucking shoot me now!" Holly yelled as another contraction hit her body.

"Language."

Holly snapped her attention to Ben. "You can take that language and shove it right up your ass."

"Young lady," Henry remarked, drawing her attention.

"Labor makes you fun," Mildred said, bouncing on her feet with delight.

The doctor looked around the room. "It was fun for a few minutes. However, I'm going to have to ask all of you to go wait in the waiting room. There's too many people and not enough room."

Holly looked around as she bit her bottom lip in pain. She couldn't agree more.

As her eyes moved around the room, she focused on the spot Jimmy had been sitting, only this time it was empty.

She scanned the room again.

A wave of panic swept through her.

He was nowhere to be found.

"Mrs. Richman, your heart rate is skyrocketing. Are you having another contraction?"

"Where's Jimmy?" She shot her eyes to Ben who also started looking around the room.

Another contraction hit her. *Fuck! No!*

The doctor took one assessment at Holly and placed his gloved hand under the sheet to check her. "It's time."

"The fuck it is!" Holly snapped her legs together effectively locking the doctor's hand in place.

"The baby is coming, Mrs. Richman."

Holly glared at him through the pain. "Let's get one thing straight here, doc." She gritted her teeth. "I'm not pushing a watermelon outta my hoo-ha until I know where my son is."

"Mrs. Richman, while you're still having the contraction you need to push."

With all her strength she held her legs together pulling herself up to the doctor at her waist. She didn't know how but she was able to grab his scrubs pulling him close. "This kid isn't gonna see the light of day until my son is in front of me. You get me?"

"That's my girl! Show that doctor who's boss," Mildred gleefully exclaimed fist pumping the air.

Ben was fast. In seconds, he unclasped Holly's hand from around the doctor's collar.

Holly turned to Ben, tears in her eyes as she fought her body's natural reactions to push.

"Found him!" John announced, walking Jimmy back into the room. Holly darted her attention to him, the relief of seeing him was quickly overthrown when she saw the tears in Jimmy's eyes.

Oh no, what happened? "Come here," Holly said, reaching out for Jimmy. "Baby, what's going on?"

Jimmy slowly walked into Holly's grasp. Ben ran around the bed and kneeled down next to him in seconds.

Jimmy looked up into Holly's eyes tears now flowing freely from him. "Once Peanut is born, you won't need me anymore."

"What?" Ben asked.

Jimmy started to choke up. "You'll both forget about me and send me to another home." His sobs grew louder.

Holly's whole world fell apart as she watched her son fear losing them. Had she really been that bad of a parent to Jimmy that she didn't instill in him no matter what happened he would always be theirs, no matter how many children they had? Jimmy was their son. End of story. She pulled him into her arms. "Jimmy, no, never. You are never ever going somewhere else. You are *my* son and no one will ever take you away from me."

"B-but, once Peanut is here you'll forget about me."

"We can never forget about you, squirt. When you came into our life you made it better." Ben pulled him into his arms.

"We love you, Jimmy. To us, you have always been our son, from that very first time we saw you on the camera." Holly looked at Ben. "Do you have the papers by any chance?"

Ben nodded. "Actually, I do. I stuffed them in my back pocket when your water broke." He quickly handed them to Holly.

"Put him on the bed," Holly said, scooting over so Jimmy would have room.

"Mrs. Richman, I need to advise you that this—"

Holly cut him off with a glare so evil the doctor took a step back holding his hands up.

Once Jimmy was right next to her, with Ben standing nestled next to both of them she unfolded the papers. "Do you see this here?"

Jimmy nodded.

"These are your adoption papers, baby. We were on our way into the backyard to tell you it was official when my water broke. With these documents here, you became our son. A Richman. We adopted you, squirt."

Jimmy stared at the papers for a few seconds before looking back to Holly. Tears were in his eyes but he was no longer sobbing. "Does this mean I can finally call you mom?"

Holly's heart exploded at his words. She pulled him into her arms hugging him like her life depended on it. She never thought he'd call her mom. Not with everything he'd been through, but hearing those words come out of his mouth was everything she'd always hoped for.

"Mom, mom." Jimmy flailed around. "Can't breathe."

Holly pulled back looking at him as tears fell from her eyes. "I'll never get tired of hearing that."

Jimmy smiled as he turned to Ben biting his lip. "Dad?"

"Every day for the rest of your life, kid." Ben scooped him off the bed and into his arms. "Love you."

"I love you, too, Dad."

"Oh no!" Holly yelled as another contraction hit her. This time with so much force she couldn't fight not pushing.

"That's it. We can't wait another second. Mrs. Richman, you're pushing or I *will* call for a cesarean section. You're risking your child's life."

Holly paled. How in the hell was she messing up so much already? "Let's do this."

Everyone was quickly ushered out of the room by the nurses as Ben stood at the head of the bed holding Holly's hand, giving her words of encouragement. As the contraction shot through her body Holly pushed like she'd never pushed before.

Within a few minutes, the room erupted in cries.

"Congratulations, it's a girl!"

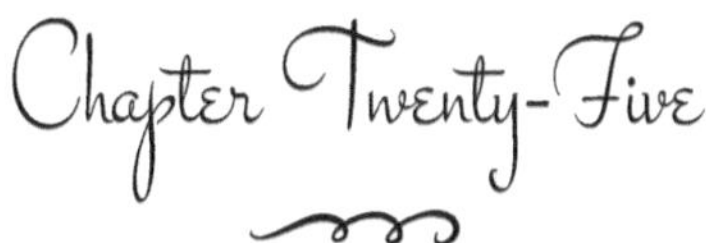

BEN HELD his daughter in his arms as his heart pounded against his chest. She was perfect in every single way possible. He never truly understood what a parent meant when they talked about the feeling of holding their child for the first time.

Now, he did.

Ben looked down at her with so much love, it was overwhelming. This was their child. Their little girl. Life couldn't get much better than this.

He looked up from his daughter to see Jimmy peacefully sleeping on the chair in the corner.

Today he was given one of the greatest gifts ever given. His children.

He looked down at this daughter one more time. *Welcome to the family, Peanut.*

Ben turned his attention to Holly. He saw her staring at him with a silly smile on her face. "She's amazing, isn't she?" she said, looking at their child in his arms.

He nodded. "Beyond any doubt."

Everyone had gone home once the baby was born leaving

just the four of them. Everything went from completely chaotic to peaceful.

He looked back at his baby girl, tears in his eyes. "Thank you." Ben turned his attention back to Holly.

She beamed at him as a lazy smile appeared on her face. "I love you, Ben."

"I love you too, Grace." He moved his attention back to the little girl in his arms.

"Do you think she'll have your eyes?" Holly asked, looking at him.

"I hope she has yours."

"There you two are," Henry said, shuffling into the room with a cup of coffee in his hand.

Ben looked to the door. "I thought John took you home?"

"I told him I called a cab." Henry shrugged.

"You lied to him?"

"An omittance of truth." Henry handed Ben the cup of coffee. "Figured you needed this."

"Thanks." He took it before placing it on the table next to him.

Henry walked over to the side of the bed kissing Holly on the cheek. "You did good, Pumpkin."

Holly smiled at him. "Thanks, Dad."

Holly turned to Ben reaching out her hands asking for the baby. Carefully, Ben stood before walking to Holly placing their baby girl in her arms.

"Dad," Holly said, holding up their child for him to see. "I would like for you to meet Helen Richman."

Henry took a step back. "Holly?"

She started nodding her head as tears appeared in her eyes.

"You didn't?"

Holly wiped away the tears falling down her cheeks. "Ben and I talked about it. If we had a boy we were going to name him after his father, a girl, mom." Holly looked down at their baby. "She looks exactly like a Helen if you ask me."

Ben plopped his hip on the bed placing his arms around Holly's shoulder cradling her and the baby in his arms. "She does. She looks *exactly* like a Helen."

"I—I don't know what to say," Henry stammered, staring at all of them as tears formed in his eyes.

"Would you like to hold your granddaughter?" Holly asked, holding her up.

"You don't have to ask me twice." Henry as quick as he could ran over to Ben's vacated chair and plopped onto it. As best as he could he positioned himself to safely hold Peanut.

Once Ben saw he was ready, he gently took Peanut from Holly and placed her in Henry's arms.

When she was situated Ben went back to Holly placing his arm around her, holding her tightly.

Here in the room was everything he ever dreamed of.

Jimmy slept soundly in the corner, officially their adopted child.

Henry held their daughter.

And he had Holly in his arms.

Ben shook his head. If two years ago, someone told him this is where he would be in his life, he would have laughed at them. But now, now he couldn't see his life any other way.

Ben looked at Holly, her smile spread from ear to ear, which he knew matched his own.

He knew his heart felt full when Jimmy came into their life, but this. This was different.

This was beyond a fullness.

This was perfect.

He leaned over kissing Holly lightly on the lips. "I love you."

She smiled back at him. "Not as much as I love you."

"I'm your grandpa, Peanut," Henry cooed, drawing Ben's

attention away from Holly. "I've waited a long time for your mom to give me grandbabies. And in one day she gave me two."

Ben watched as Henry spoke to their daughter.

"I'm the cool Grandpa," he stated. "I'll always be there for you whenever you need me. I'll be here. For you *and* your brother."

"The cool grandpa, really?" Holly laughed.

Henry looked at her. "You know it. I'll make it my mission to stay up on the trends."

"Oh, this is gonna be fun." Ben laughed along with Holly.

"I can learn those texting machines if I need to, or the internet box. I can do it."

Ben chuckled.

Yep, this *was* perfect.

Henry turned back to Peanut. "She's beautiful."

"She is," Ben agreed. "Just as beautiful as Holly."

"Thank you for naming her after your mother." Henry caressed Peanut's cheek.

"There was never a doubt," Holly answered.

Henry looked up at them with a new twinkle in his eyes, as his lopsided grin appeared. "You know, she definitely came into this world with a bang."

"That's Holly's MO." Ben pulled his wife closer. "I was a little worried for the doctor there at one point."

"Me too."

"Hey, you don't get between a mother and her children." Holly crossed her arms over her chest.

Ben leaned over kissing her hairline. "You've always had that possessive gene in you, Grace. I pity anyone that tries you."

Henry's chuckle went through the room. "And you have Mildred on your side. She's a force to be reckoned with. I can still hear her taking bets on if Peanut was gonna be a boy or girl." Henry shook his head. "You know, she was trying to hustle the staff, right?"

"I'm not the least bit surprised," Ben answered.

"I'm still not sure how her husband doesn't murder her," Holly replied, closing her eyes.

"Love is funny that way, isn't it?" Henry looked back down at Helen before turning back to them. "How do you two feel?"

"Amazing," they said in unison.

Henry smiled back at them. "It's a wonderful feeling, right?"

"It is."

"There is one thing I can't wait for, though," Henry said, giving them both a lopsided grin.

"And what's that?" Ben asked, cocking his head to the side.

"Introducing Peanut to Lord Waffles."

Chapter Twenty-Six

FIVE MONTHS LATER

LIFE WAS A FUCKING CHAOTIC MESS.

But Holly wouldn't have it any other way.

It might have been a mess, but it was her mess, and she'd never been happier.

Holly looked around her living room. On the floor, Jimmy was wrestling with Ripley, with Twitch trying to hold his own. In the corner of the room, Waffles was climbing up the cat tree looking for treats.

Peanut was crying so Ben was rocking her in his arms.

And the whole room looked like it had exploded with toys —human and dog, clothes, blankets, and food. You name it. It was in her living room.

Still, even through all that, Holly had a goofy smile on her face.

Glancing around her home she noticed Waffles had made it to the second level on the cat tree. With a deep sigh, she pushed her three-day unwashed hair out of her face and made her way over to him. She plucked him from the cat tree and placed him on the floor, much to his protest.

Waffles stared up at her in disgust as he huffed loudly at her.

"What did you do to him?" Ben asked, coming over to Holly. Peanut still in his arms as she cried.

"I took him off the cat tree." Holly wiped off the front of her shirt. There were vomit stains, and something else, but she wasn't quite sure what it was. She decided it was best to ignore it.

"Did I forget to put the gate around it again?" Ben asked, looking behind her at Waffles.

"No, you did. He thinks when there's madness going on, he can get away with pushing it to the side."

"Typical Waffles."

"Never a dull moment."

Jimmy's laughter rang throughout the room as he continued to play with Ripley and Twitch. He kept squeaking one of the dog toys driving Ripley to bark.

Then Peanut started to cry louder.

Holly caught Ben's eye. Simultaneously a smile spread across their faces.

Chaos never looked so good.

Ben leaned forward kissing Holly on the cheek. "Love you, Grace."

"Love you more."

"I'm gonna take this one to the nursery and see if I can get her down for a nap."

"Good luck." He was gonna need it.

"If it works, you and I are sneaking off to the bedroom for five minutes."

Holly's eyes brightened. "That's all you're gonna give me, big guy? Five minutes."

Ben growled at her causing Holly to throw her head back and laugh.

"I bet I can make you come no less than three times and still have a minute to spare," he whispered into her ear.

"Talk is cheap."

"Oh, Grace. You're gonna get it."

"Maybe."

Ben kissed her again. "Be ready." He turned on his heel making his way down the hall with Peanut still crying.

Never a dull moment.

She'd give Ben a few minutes before she sent Jimmy out back with the pups to play.

Hell, five minutes was all she needed.

Holly walked to the kitchen and reached for her trusted donut box. Once she had it, she took out her prized possession.

That's when she noticed Waffles plop down on his butt staring her down as he eyed what was in her hand.

Not surprising, Waffles then lunged for her treat. Holly was too quick for him this time, though. She yanked it away from him. Waffles plopped back on the floor sending her a severe side-eye.

Holly took a bite as she laughed. "Not this time, Waffles."

Waffles huffed in annoyance.

"This peanut butter glazed donut is mine!"

Just then Ripley came running into the kitchen with Jimmy chasing after her. Holly being completely taken off guard, tried swerving away but ended up losing her footing.

Before Holly knew it, she was on the floor staring at the ceiling.

That's when Waffles casually walked over to her and plucked the donut from her grasp.

He looked down at her as he happily chomped on the last bite.

Instead of fighting it, Holly rested her head on the kitchen floor.

She counted to five the moment she heard Ben's footsteps.

"Holy shit. What happened? I leave you for two minutes and you're already on the floor," he asked, dropping to his knees checking her out before helping Holly to her feet.

"Waffles. Waffles is what happened."

Once Holly was fully upright, Ben shook his head. "That's it."

Holly knitted her brows together as she watched Ben leave the kitchen in a huff and head into their garage.

"What are you doing?" she called out.

When he reappeared in the kitchen he held up his hand. "It's time to try the bubble wrap again."

HOLLY AND BEN *now* have a Holiday story! Check it out in ***Stumbling Into the Holidays!***

Stay connected to find out when **John and Emma's** story will be released.

CURIOUS WHAT MILDRED was talking about when she saw a hunky firefighter and his woman in a compromising position? Check out Hank and Olive's story in Teased by Fire. Sneak peek of Chapter One next.

CHAPTER ONE

OLIVE QUINN GLARED daggers at her traitorous best friend, Miranda Parker, as the bane of her existence—Hank Parker—moved yet another piece of his furniture into her apartment.

"Stop trying to murder me with your eyes, Olive." Miranda sighed with a huff of annoyance as she pushed the hair out of her face.

That only caused Olive to glare harder in her friend's direction. "I will *not* stop trying to murder you with my eyes," Olive whisper shouted. "It's your fault *he* is moving into *my* apartment."

"What the hell did you want me to do, Olive? I knew I couldn't leave you stranded to pay the rent on your own. You're just pissed I'm moving."

"Damn right, I'm pissed. If I were you, I'd check every box you packed for surprises." Olive squinted her eyes harder in Miranda's direction trying to intimidate her.

"How many times are we going to go through this?" Miranda shook her head. "If I thought I had a chance of getting the job, I would've told you. I legit figured hell would've frozen over before they offered me the position."

"And yet here we are. Hell must be mighty cold right now."

"I'm sorry, okay. I'm freaking sorry."

At Miranda's defeated posture Olive softened. "No, I'm the one that's sorry. You've got your dream job now. I need to stop being angry and just be happy for you."

"It's a lot of things changing all at once."

Olive looked at Miranda, her eyes filling with tears. "I'm going to miss you. We've been stuck together since the first grade."

"Nothing's changing," Miranda tried reassuring her.

"Everything is changing. You're moving clear across the country and I only found out two days ago. I haven't had time to accept the fact my only friend is leaving me." Her eyes narrowed. "And, to top it all off, you went behind my back and gave your *brother* your room."

Miranda sighed before crossing her arms over her chest. "I don't understand why you are freaking out so much. Yeah, Hank is an ass, but if you both stay out of each other's way, you'll be fine. Plus, I've brought you the best research tool a romance writer could ever ask for. You'll be able to get up close and personal experience on how he operates. I brought you a gift."

"If you mean the gift of an STI infested manwhore? You can keep it." Olive's eyes widened as everything clicked into place. *Oh my God!* This wasn't her best friend. Nope. There was no way in hell *her* best friend—who she'd known for years—would actually be doing this. There was only one explanation. Miranda had been abducted by aliens and the person standing in front of her was an imposter.

This is it. This is the zombie apocalypse we've all been waiting for.

Olive quickly grabbed Miranda's arms, examining them for any sign of an implant.

"Jesus, Olive, what are you doing?" Miranda instantly snatched her hands back.

"Checking to see if you have a tracking device somewhere," she stated as a matter of fact.

Miranda rolled her eyes. "Do you ever live anywhere other than your fantasy world?"

Offended, Olive crossed her arms over her chest. "Hey, my weird brain is a masterpiece. How else do you think I come up with my stories?"

"I don't know how you function when all you think about is the zombie apocalypse or some strange alien race invading the earth."

Olive pointed at her head. "This imagination makes me money."

"How? Your brain makes zero sense. Besides you don't even write the shit that goes on in your mind." Miranda shook her head. "Olive, you write contemporary erotic romance. Please explain to me how a brain so involved in aliens and zombies writes hardcore romance with alpha males who make all women drool?"

Olive shrugged. "I don't know. I think it's a weird yin and yang thing. You know, balance to the Force and what not."

"Fuck!" They heard from the other room as a loud bang echoed throughout the space.

Olive's eyes narrowed back at her friend as her lips thinned. "He's a big oaf, and he's gonna use his big oaf muscles to make holes in my walls."

Miranda crossed her arms over her chest. "All right, Olive, I get it. You're fucking pissed. Okay. If I were you I'd be pissed too, but there is nothing we can do about it now. Hank is moving in. Right now, as we speak. He needed a place and you need someone that can pay half the rent. End. Of. Story."

Olive knew Miranda was right, but that didn't stop the betrayal and hurt from running through her. Within two days, everything she was accustomed to had been upended. That's a lot for anyone to take in.

"It's not like he'll be here often anyway," Miranda remarked. "He's always at the fire station, and when he's not, he'll be out with his flavor of the week."

"That isn't the point. With Hank the Tank..." Olive physically revolted. "I hate that nickname everyone calls him."

"I agree, it's stupid."

"Back to what I was saying," Olive started again after shaking the thoughts from her head. "With Hank moving in, I can't be me anymore. Olive Quinn: awkward, hates people, never goes outside or wears a bra. I'll be banished to my room or *forced* to wear a bra. I don't want to wear a bra. Bras suck and stifle my creativity. Oh God, don't even get me started on underwires. Who the hell came up with underwires for bras, anyway? I bet you it was a man. Yup, it had to have been a man. A woman wouldn't have invented something that after a little while a hard metal wire pokes out and causes you excruciating pain." She grunted. "All you want to do is walk to the store and buy some snacks. But *nooo*, instead I'm walking down the sidewalk discreetly trying to move the wire to a place where it's not trying to puncture through my skin and kill me."

Miranda chuckled as she shook her head. "You have a point about the bra, but you said the same thing about pants and you've grown accustomed to wearing them."

"*Not by choice!* I only wear them because you kept the air on 'cold as fuck.' If I didn't wear pants these thunder thighs would have gotten frostbitten."

"I keep it cold because you have that weird obsession with the holidays."

"I do not!"

Miranda's brow rose before she pointed to the corner of Olive's bedroom. "You have a freakin' Christmas tree up."

"Yeah, what's your point?"

"It's the middle of *June*. No one needs a Christmas tree up in the middle of June."

Olive held her hand to her chest as if she'd been shot. "How can you say that?"

Miranda instantly rolled her eyes. "It's the *middle of June*. That's how I can say that."

"Haven't you heard of Christmas in July? I'm just a few weeks early."

"Christmas in July," Miranda scoffed. "Olive, you haven't taken it down in the three years we've lived here."

"Damn, Scrooge much? Sorry, my joy of the holidays makes you a bitter humbug."

Miranda held Olive's shoulders. "Please leave this apartment more often and get some fresh air. I really am worried about you."

"Do not shit all over my love of the happiest time of the year. And, stop deflecting on the fact that *you* went behind my back and moved in your brother."

"Think of all the material you'll get for your books now." Miranda swiped her hand toward the bedroom door. "His friends are delicious. What more could you ask for? Hot firemen as your personal research subjects. You can save your computer from all the viruses from those porn sites you…" She made air quotes. "…use for research."

"Hey, don't knock it. Those sites are a golden tool for my line of work."

"Whatever. It's done. Now, let's go back out there and get the rest of my stuff packed away."

Olive huffed before following her friend. "Remember those *research subjects* include your brother the next time you read one of my books." Olive couldn't help the smirk that spread across her face when Miranda's eyes widened. *Take that you, traitorous devil woman!*

"Oh shit, what have I done?"

Olive pushed Miranda's shoulder, shoving her toward the door. "Serves you right."

As they walked back into the living room, Olive's heart stopped as she saw a shirtless, sweaty Hank standing in the middle of the room. How in the hell was it possible to look *that* good? He had muscles for days. Her eyes went to his abs as she started mentally counting them. Sure, half the men in her books were described like him, but that was in her mind. Men did *not* look like them in real life. And why the hell was he looking at her like she was a tall glass of water and he was a man dying of thirst?

Her whole body shivered. She one-hundred percent stepped into an alternate universe.

"There you two are," Hank remarked. "I thought you'd left all the work to us." He nodded his head toward his station buddies who'd agreed to help move Miranda out and him in.

Olive looked around at the men scattered throughout the room. It was like a *Hot Fireman/Paramedic* calendar threw up in her apartment.

Maybe this wasn't such a bad idea after all.

She turned toward her friend and smirked, which made Miranda blanch for a brief second before she spoke. "No, we haven't left. We were just discussing something in Olive's room," Miranda announced before making her way to one of the many boxes in the living room.

"That so. And what did you and Olive Oil need to discuss?" Hank smirked in her direction.

"Do not call me that!" Olive glanced around the room for something to throw at his head. She'd grown up with Hank teasing her every chance he got, and if he thought she would just stand by and let him do it in her own home, he had another thing coming.

At her annoyance, Hank chuckled. "Oh, I think living with you will be lots of fun, Olive Oil."

Olive turned back to Miranda ready to demand she make him leave when Hank yelled out, "Any of you seen Dog?"

A chorus of *no's* rang out throughout the room which made Olive roll her eyes. "Let me guess, another one of your degenerate friends?" she asked, glaring at Hank.

His eyes brightened with laughter as his smile grew wider. "Miranda didn't tell you about Dog?"

Olive's eyes shot to her best friend who was now pretending to remove an invisible piece of dirt from her shirt. "No, I guess that tidbit of information escaped her," Olive sneered.

Hank disappeared out of the room leaving Olive with her brow raised and her arms crossed at his sudden departure. *Well, okay then. Clearly living with Hank was not going to be a walk in the park.*

A few minutes later she heard Hank shout, "Found her!" He then made his way back into the living room. That's when Olive spotted the largest Maine Coon cat she'd ever seen in her life cradled in Hank's arms.

"What is that?"

Hank scratched the cat on its head causing the ginormous creature to tilt its face in his direction seeking out more attention, or possibly meat from a small animal being used as a sacrifice. "This is Dog," he said with a grin.

That's when she snapped. "Who the fuck names a *cat* Dog?"

CONTINUE HANK and Olive's story In Teased by Fire.

Also by Molly O'Hare

Stumbling Through Life Series

Stumbling Into Him

Stumbling Into Forever

Stumbling Into the Holidays

John & Emma's story – *Coming soon*

Teased by Love Series

Teased by Fire

Teased by Tinsel

Lucas & Miranda's story – Coming soon

Hollywood Hopeful Series

Hollywood Dreams

Risking It All (Danny and Lexi's Story) – *Coming soon*

Standalone Novels

Nothing But a Dare

Learning Curves

Stay Connected

Sign up for my newsletter or check out my website.

If you just want to hang out, come join my reader group: Molly's Badass Babes.

About the Author

Molly O'Hare is a USA Today Bestselling author of curvy romance books.

She's obsessed with all things animals, mainly Corgis, and body positivity. She grew up with severe dyslexia: trust her, spelling is not her strong suit. Over the years, she's become a huge advocate of "just because you learn something a little differently than others doesn't make you less." To help herself fall asleep, she'd create stories in her head, always picking up where she left off the night before. Molly figured if she got enjoyment out of her imagination, others might as well. So here we are.

To find out more or sign up for her newsletter, check out her social page on her website: https://www.mollyohareauthor.com/social-page/

I think I will bestow upon you some fun facts about me.

Fun Facts for Stumbling Into Forever:

I *still* have a Corgi.

I hate donuts.

I love car rides.

I love foxes.

I tripped *into* the car this morning.

I sing at the top of my lungs. Especially, if I *don't* know the words.

Stay Connected

www.ingramcontent.com/pod-product-compliance
Lightning Source LLC
Chambersburg PA
CBHW021148110726
47900CB00002B/476